THE ASTOUNDING MISADVENTURES OF RORY COLLINS

THE
ASTOUNDING
MISADVENTURES
OF RORY
COLLINS

BRIAN KILEY

Distributed by
Argo Navis Author Services
www.argonavisdigital.com

Print ISBN: 978-0-7867-5620-9
ebook ISBN: 978-0-7867-5621-6

Distributed by Argo Navis Author Services

CONTENTS

ACKNOWLEDGMENTS

This is the part of a book that I never read. This and the "notes." I hate the notes. However, this is my first book and it has made me realize why this part is necessary. You don't write a book all by yourself. I don't any way. There are people along the way who listened and gave notes and encouraged and I am truly indebted to them.

First off, I have to thank Paula Killen who was the first to tell me that this wasn't a short story and that I had a book in me. I'd also like to thank Jane Morris for all her insight and encouragement. I'd like to thank Drew Brody, Kathy Boutry, Chris Pearson, Matt Lopez, Laura Burns and Joe Brouillette, all real friends and real writers.

I'd like to thank everyone in Write Club who listened to this story unfold each week, Rosemary Vaswani, Clara York, Virginia Watson, Exetta Harris, James Schneider, Gordon Henderson, Jessica Williamson, Ramsey Brown, Becky Wahlstrom, Lauri Fraser, Kristi Israel, Susan Vaughn, Jim Rasfeld, Bill Jenkins, Kate O'Neil, Kim Rome, Debra Olson Tolar, Hutch Foster, Erika Greene, Bess Fanning, Antonio Sacre and the late great Jay Leggett.

I'd also like to thank my two former managers Leah Hoyer and Ava Greenfield, both of whom selfishly I wish hadn't moved on to better things. I'd also like to thank Steve Fisher and the good people at APA. I'd like to thank the incomparable Barry Crimmins, my friend and mentor who has been after me for years to write a novel.

Finally, I'd to thank my pals, my wife Sandy and my son Sean and daughter Ali (who I hope don't read this until they're 40) And since no one is reading this part anyway, I'd also like to thank Carl Yastrzemski for no particular reason.

ONE

Missing your mother's funeral is not like missing a flight where you can catch the next one. It's not like missing the Super Bowl where a year later you can see something quite similar. Your mother's funeral is a once in a lifetime event that provides the family with a sense of comfort and closure. Without it, there's a permanent sense of discomfort and whatever the opposite of closure is.

The truth is there was no good reason for us to miss it. We thought the funeral was at ten. It was at nine. I had arrived home from college the night before and I was up early after having fitful dreams about my newly dead mother. My father got up early like he always did. We had a leisurely breakfast of tea and toast. There were long periods of silence where I thought some things should be said but I didn't know what "things." "What would normal people say in this situation?" I wondered. When he got his coat, I got mine and we walked mostly single file through streets narrowed by graying snow to the church we never attended.

At the time of my mother's death in 1982, I was a sophomore at Philbin College. It's about thirty miles west of Philadelphia. It was named for Colonel Wesby Philbin, a textile magnate, who lost his right hand during the battle of Gettysburg while fighting for the Confederacy. Long Story.

I found out she had died two days after her death. I had just walked out of Psych class and found my roommate Todd waiting for me with a strange expression on his face.

"Sorry, dude," he said softly.

I went right to the station and hopped the first train home. She had just turned forty-four earlier that week and as far as I knew she hadn't been sick.

I grew up in a small town in the part of Pennsylvania where people mind their own business. I was always pretty sure my mother loved me although I had little evidence to support my theory. My first memories of her were when I was little and I would run around the house or honk the horn of my toy car and she would yell, "Quiet!" The whole time I knew her she would demand silence from my father and me. She had a habit of sitting and staring straight ahead. Often in the middle of an activity, she could be cooking or cleaning or eating and she would suddenly stop what she was doing and go and sit in the faded red chair in the living room, focus on a spot on the wall and become lost in thought. This might last anywhere from just a few minutes to most of the afternoon.

Some days, after lunch, she would go up to her bedroom and come back down with a notebook in her hand. She would sit in her chair, open it up and become instantly inspired. She would write furiously never stopping to find the right word or clarify a thought. She would write at a frenzied pace for five or ten minutes then abruptly stop and close her notebook. Pulling herself out of her chair she would quickly move up the stairs with a curious urgency while clutching the notebook tightly to her bosom.

Her writing sessions only occurred after lunch and never when my father was home, something I failed to notice as a child. Her thinking sessions, however, might happen any time. During these periods, my father and I learned to tiptoe and whisper and we made sure not to cross her field of vision. When the phone rang in these instances, she would scream, "They ruined it", head to her bedroom and slam the door while my father dealt with whoever was on the phone.

When it came time for kindergarten, my mother just kept me home. It wasn't exactly "home schooling" since no such trend existed at that time and she didn't teach me anything. In fact, we barely interacted at all unless she was knitting a large garment and needed me to model it for her.

The following year, my mother would have had me stay home again but my father gently mentioned during one of our many silent meals that it was time to sign the boy up for school. She did so reluctantly and thereafter drove me the three short blocks every morning.

After a few weeks, he told her that this was unnecessary and that the boy could use some exercise. They often called me "the boy" instead of "Rory" and spoke in front of me as though I were a puppy or an inanimate object incapable of comprehending human conversation.

I began walking to school on my own. However, my mother, for the rest of my grammar school career, would follow slowly behind in the car. If one of my classmates approached me or an older student made a move to pass me along the sidewalk, she would beep the horn long and loud until they scurried away.

Somehow, I still managed to make a few friends, but I was never allowed to accept invitations to what kids nowadays call, "playdates." Thanks to my father's gentle but persistent prodding, eventually some boys, one at a time of course, were allowed to come to my house after school. My mother hated when I had a friend over even though my two closest friends Doug and Stevie learned to tiptoe outside with me if one of my Mom's "thinking sessions" broke out. She often ignored us almost pretending we weren't there. At other times, she would become irritable and shoo us outside regardless of the weather. She behaved this way again and again in front of each of my friends. Until the day I brought home Derek.

We were nine and Derek and his family had moved here from the south, Mississippi or Alabama, I can never remember which. When Derek came in the door, my mother instantly stopped what she was doing and introduced herself. This was unprecedented. She poured us milk and gave us cookies, handing Derek his like a priest handing out communion. Once or twice, she called him, "George."

"His name is Derek," I said.

It rained that day so Derek and I stayed in and sat on the floor in my room playing a board game I had called "The Secret Agent." My mother brought in a chair from her bedroom, placed it alongside Derek and gently stroked his hair while we played. He didn't seem to mind or notice really. Girls were always fawning all over him.

For the next several weeks, when I asked if I could have Doug or Stevie or perhaps someone new over my mother would say, "Why would you want to play them when you could play with Derek?"

Sometimes when the school day ended, I would find my mother outside waiting for us and she would invite Derek over. She had taken up baking for the first time and made tollhouse cookies for Derek until she discovered he preferred brownies.

Once outside the school, Derek's Mom was there to pick him up and bring him to a dentist appointment. She and my Mom got into a loud argument when my Mom suggested that they reschedule Derek's appointment for another day.

"Derek doesn't need to go to the dentist," my mother insisted, "He has beautiful teeth."

At the end of the school year, Derek's family moved back to Mississippi or Alabama. When I told my mother this during dinner that night she abruptly stopped eating. She put the fork down with half a meatball still impaled on it, went to her bedroom and closed the door. For two days, even through the night, loud, full-throated sobs came from behind that closed door and my father had to sleep on a cot in the sewing room.

When she finally emerged from her room we were forbidden to ever mention Derek's name again and things went on as before. My life continued and to the outside world, things seemed normal enough in my house and because I didn't know any better they seemed normal enough for me. The one large void in my life at that time (other than love and affection which I didn't know I was missing) was birthday parties. I had never once been to one.

As you can imagine birthday parties are a frequent topic of conversation in the primary grades. I heard talk of bowling and swimming pools and piñatas. Sometimes a boy in my class would have a party and ask me why I wasn't there. When I asked my mother about an invitation in the mail, she would shrug and say she didn't know what I was talking about. Once or twice a year, the phone rang and I was sure it was Doug or Stevie's Mom calling to see if I was coming. My mother would take the call in the other room and then afterwards say it was an old relative of hers calling to share some family business and the birthday party would come and go without me.

When I was thirteen, a party invitation arrived on a Saturday and my father was there to discover it. My mother said, "Absolutely not"; it was a girl/boy party. When I pleaded my father settled the dispute in my favor saying, "It would be good for the boy." The evening of the party, my mother drove me silently to the house. We parked out front and as she was giving me rendezvous instructions, a girl from my class, Lisa Metcalf walked in front of our car. Lisa's hair was done up, she had a touch of make-up around her eyes and her small breasts were pushed up to their full height.

My mother muttered, "She thinks she's so pretty" and I involuntarily blurted out, "She is."

My mother slapped me hard across the face and I started crying not because I was injured but out of shame.

We went right home and when we walked in the door my father looked up from his book with a surprised expression. My mother said, "He decided he didn't want to go" and that was the end of that.

These were the memories that were in my head as the train pulled into the station. I could see my father waiting for me on the platform in the distance. It occurred to me that I must be in shock because I hadn't cried a single tear. As I approached, I saw that his face seemed without emotion and anyone observing us would never suspect we were in the midst of a family tragedy.

"What happened?" I asked.

TWO

When my father met me at the train station he seemed small to me. After three and a quarter semesters at college, I had become used to large people. My roommate Todd, the one I slept in the same room with, was a starting lineman on our school's football team. Dale, one of my other roommates, claimed repeatedly to have been a star basketball player in high school. Even my pedantic roommate Kevin was a flabby two hundred-pounder.

Now, looking at my father it occurred to me for the first time that I could take this guy in a fight. His back seemed slightly stooped, his movements slow and cautious and with his limited vision, the fight would probably be stopped in the second or third round.

When I asked what had happened, he quietly mumbled, "her heart stopped," before turning and shuffling the three blocks to the funeral home. I had no more questions and I followed him as he walked so slowly and cautiously over the icy sidewalks I nearly bumped into him once or twice.

My Dad was eighteen years older than my Mom. Even as a young child I was well aware that my father was older than my friends' fathers. In the first grade, each of us had to draw a picture of our Dad for Father's Day.

Rachel Tompkins asked me, "Why is your Dad's hair gray?"

I didn't know. All I knew was that I wished it were brown like her Dad's.

Whenever my father tried to carry in too much firewood my mother would say, "Go help your father before he has a heart attack. Don't be so selfish." Once my mother introduced this threat of a heart attack it became a rational fear that took up space in my mind next to my irrational ones. Rational fears are worse because those are the ones you never outgrow.

Whenever my father overexerted himself, shoveling too much snow or climbing more than two flights of stairs his breath would become labored and my stomach would knot up and I'd think, "This is it." Even after he caught his breath, it would be hours or even days before I could relax again.

The threat of his death being constant it never occurred to me that she might die and I'm guessing it hadn't occurred to him either. Now, suddenly, we both were thrust into a situation we had never envisioned and neither of us knew what to say or do.

It would be another seven years before I would learn that my mother had taken her own life and longer than that before I discovered it was my fault. Technically, her heart had stopped. Yours would too if you'd taken a shotgun and blown off the side of your head.

This was one of the many parts of the story he had left out. I was unused to my father lying. He had always been straight forward even with bad news in his quiet, gentle way. This was only time I can recall him lying to me my whole life and I can't say I blame him.

When we reached the funeral home parking lot and we were able to walk two abreast once more, my father described how the wake had been.

"It was a wonderful tribute, a wonderful tribute," he insisted.

His former business partner had showed up with his wife. Three of my old teachers and Miss Gillen, my former guidance counselor had put in an appearance. Even Doug, my former grade school chum had come, in an altered state no doubt, to acknowledge a bond that was frayed but never entirely severed.

With perhaps one or two more attendees, the grand total must have reached eight or even nine. Not bad for a woman without friends and whose feuds with extended family were complete and unrelenting.

The funeral director, Mr. Haus was smaller than my father and nearly as old. "I could take him, too" I thought as we shook hands and he offered me perfunctory condolences. "The funeral will be at Our Lady of Perpetual Help," Mr. Haus informed us and he had taken the liberty of asking the ladies of the St. Patrick Society to sing the hymns.

I eyed my father obliquely. Although our last name was Collins, both my parents were not Irish but Polish. My father's grandfather's name Collesnewicz had been Anglicized or in this case, Celticized at Ellis Island and people have assumed we were Irish ever since. Eventually, I learned it was easier to wear green every St. Patrick's Day than to have to explain over and over the clerical procedures concerning Central European immigrants.

"The ladies of the St. Patrick Society…" my father said softly, "That would be lovely." I'll never know if the debacle that occurred the next morning was the fault of Mr. Haus or of the Collins, nee Collesnewicz.

I rose early the next morning, showered and shaved and put on the suit I wore when I testified during her trial my junior year of high school. I had grown an inch or two since then and when I put it on it didn't quite fit right.

I remember how cold it was walking to her funeral. I shivered and my Dad nodded in agreement continuing a lifelong tradition of mostly non-verbal communication. I could see the church steeple in the distance and I felt both relief and uneasiness the closer we got. By the time we reached the church parking lot I found myself sweating in spite of the cold.

As we started up the church steps, the double doors swung open and eight or nine ladies of mature age, all clad in green, exited the church. The last one, with fading red hair and a back-up chin just in case, stopped suddenly upon seeing my father. While we were still several steps away she blurted out, "Where the hell were you?"

THREE

Since my mother's funeral was on a Thursday, the nine people who came to her wake all had to go to work the next morning. Aside from the ladies of the St. Patrick's Society and the priest, no one came to her funeral. Not even her husband. Not even her son.

When Colonel Philbin died, the entire town shut down. The mill closed for the day so that all the workers, mostly recent immigrants, could attend the funeral. Hundreds of people came. The vice-president sent a telegram.

Colonel Philbin's horse, Old Nat, had been shot out from under him at Gettysburg. Afterwards, promoting his own legend, Philbin named each subsequent horse, "Old Nat". The final "Old Nat" pulled the carriage carrying his coffin, riderless, down Main Street while men and women wept publicly. My mother had her faults but she never owned slaves.

At the Irish woman's blunt, "Where the hell were you?" my father and I stood immobilized a dozen or so steps from the church doors. Seconds or possibly minutes later, my father mumbled, "The service is at ten." This was met with a laugh and a "I've got news for you, Buster" as the Irish woman came straight at us.

"The mass was at nine and you just missed it."

She stopped at the step above my father. Her face resting comfortably on her chins seemed accusatory rather than sympathetic.

There was a brief stand-off. Then my father murmured, "Thank you," and he circled around her and headed up the steps. Her disdainful look then fell to me. She was acting as if we were her children and we had deliberately missed her funeral. Duly chastened, I put my head down and slipped past her.

I followed behind my father as he moved purposely through the empty church, knocking before entering the sacristy. Father Barrett was just removing his surplus.

Our family didn't go to church so I didn't know Father Barrett very well but I had seen him around town and ironically, once or twice, I watched him preside over a funeral. He wasn't one of those touchy-feely priests from the late sixties. He was one of those manly World War II priests, gruff and barrel-chested with a ruddy, capillary-strewn face.

When we entered, Barrett turned sharply and looked at my father and then at me.

"Oh, there you are" he said, "We tried to wait for you. We even started ten minutes late." "We thought it started at ten," my father stammered.

Like the Irish woman moments earlier, Barrett shook his massive head.

"Our funeral masses are always at nine."

"Could you do it again?" I said, jumping in trying to share in my father's shame.

"There are no do-overs," Barrett said gently but without compassion.

Aside from being the pastor at Our Lady of Perpetual Help, Barrett was also the principal of the parochial school. The term "do-over" was one he had probably heard many times on the playground but it sounded funny coming from him.

"I'm due to distribute communion at the nursing home and then I'm meeting the bishop for lunch. Thursdays are our busiest day."

"What about tomorrow?" I said, desperate to salvage something from the wreckage, "Could you do it again tomorrow?"

"Tomorrow, I'm saying mass for the parochial school. First Friday, you know."

We didn't know. We didn't know a fucking thing.

Neither my father nor I had any more suggestions. Barrett softened a little, "I can give you my notes from the sermon if you like and show you the readings and the gospel."

"That would be lovely," my father said, "Could we sit in a pew and look them over and say some prayers."

Barrett hesitated.

"Only for about ten minutes. I have to go and it's not safe to leave the church unlocked. This town has vandals, you know."

Days later, I wondered if that "vandals" remark was a dig at my mother.

My Dad thanked Barrett and the two of us sat in the front pew, each with a prayer book reading the scripture to ourselves. We read how it was dust in which we began and dust into which we'd be returning. Barrett's "notes" were not much of anything, a handful of partial sentences of the generic loving mother/devoted wife variety. He obviously had no idea what this woman was really about.

Neither of us said much on the long walk home. The shock of her death was compounded by the guilt of missing her funeral. I wasn't a psychology major, I was a history major but like any college student I was familiar with something called "a Freudian slip." Two weeks earlier, Professor Jelinak had explained that forgetting something can be a version of a Freudian slip. He used the example of the man with the toothache who keeps forgetting to call and make an appointment with the dentist. He forgets because his subconscious is afraid of the dentist and doesn't want to go.

Did I forget on purpose? Did Haus say the funeral was at nine and I blocked it out? During the last few years, my mother and my relationship had degenerated from love/hate to hate/hate. Did I do this? Did I cause my father to miss his wife's funeral?

When we got home, my father sat in the living room in my mother's faded red chair. It must have made him feel closer to her by sitting in her chair. I sat nearby on the couch. We sat in silence he with his grief and me with my guilt. I could feel his angst with each of his long staccato sighs, one of which was interrupted by Mary Ann calling to offer condolences and tell me that she was pregnant.

FOUR

Mary Ann was my first real girlfriend depending or not if you count Diane. At the time of her phone call, Mary Ann and I had met only once and now she was pregnant. My relationship with Diane lasted for less than one day and ended, before our first kiss, with my mother's arrest and subsequent trial. Say what you will about my affairs but they are not uneventful. I'll never be part of those couples who at their 50th high school reunion can't quite remember if they actually dated or merely flirted way back when. The details of my liaisons are forever seared into our collective souls.

Diane and I were in the same honors English class all four years of high school. She had a round face that made her look pudgy and pudgy calves that made her look round. Her nose was small and slightly tilted to one side. Her hair was a non-descript brown with similarly colored eyes that were almost but not quite cock-eyed. She was beautiful.

I've always been an introvert. In my house, my mother did the talking. She did the talking and I did the brooding. Those were the two things we both got pretty good at especially after I got my scar, a hideous gash under my right eye that stretches from one side of the room to the other no matter what room I happen to be in.

With a personality and a scar like mine, it took years of meeting three times a week for a girl to warm up to me. By the spring of junior year, I found Diane seated next to me, on the side opposite my scar, often echoing and elaborating on my answers on the few occasions when I did raise my hand. Small talk before and after class became our normal routine.

One day in mid-autumn senior year with small town Pennsylvania showing off its foliage, Diane and I were alone on the stairway still discussing "One Flew Over the Cuckoo's Nest." She found McMurphy to be a Christ-figure which I found unlikely since to my knowledge, Jesus never swindled any mental patients. While she spoke, it suddenly occurred to me that I should ask her out. "Do it," I thought, "Do it, have some balls for once, do it." I waited patiently for her to finish making her inane point.

"Do you want to go to the movies with me on Saturday night?"

She was as surprised as I was.

"Sure," she said after a moment, "that sounds like fun."

"Kiss her," I thought, "What are you afraid of, kiss her."

I didn't dare. We left it at that and exchanging smiles walked away.

That night at dinner as we sat hammering away at our overdone pork chops, I abruptly broke the silence.

"I asked a girl to the movies on Saturday night."

My mother's head jerked violently in my direction. My father with a spoonful of mint jelly in his mouth froze.

"You did?" he asked, "What did she say?"

"She said, 'Yes.'"

My father didn't smile exactly but I did catch a twinkle in his eye as he murmured, "Isn't that something?" My mother who had been staring at me, now turned to him and then back to me again. She put down her pork chop, placed her napkin on the table, got up and went to the bathroom.

"Oh, boy," my father murmured softly to himself. A moment later, my mother was back. She returned her napkin to her lap and with renewed vigor looked me dead in the eye, "Who is this girl?"

"Her name is Diane Tracy. She's been in my honors English class for four years now and she's a very nice girl."

Any girl who finds Christ-like qualities in Jack Nicholson has to be nice I wanted to add but didn't.

"Yes" my mother continued, "But what do we really know about her?"

"Well, she's on the yearbook committee, her Dad is a dentist and all the teachers really like her."

My mother nodded and paused, "It could be an act. Sometimes a girl will"- My father delicately cut her off, "Helen, it's part of growing up. I'm proud of him."

She clenched her jaw tightly and spoke without looking at either of us.

"Well, I see there is nothing more I can say with the two of you ganging up on me."

"No one is ganging up on anyone," he said to her back as she retreated to her bedroom and closed the door.

Later that night as I sat at my desk putting the finishing touches to my essay on the Mexican-American War, I could hear the two of them arguing.

"You should have supported me," my mother yelled.

In a much softer tone, my father came back with, "Helen, the boy needs to grow up."

"You should have supported me, especially after what you put me through."

It was remark which would puzzle me for years to come.

The next morning when I came down for breakfast, my mother was still asleep. Although this was unprecedented given the fight the night before I thought little of it. My mind was pleasantly preoccupied with daydreams of Saturday night. English was my first class that morning and electricity pulsed through me all the way to school.

Diane met me at the door of our classroom. She had been crying, her eyes were puffy and red and her hair was uncombed for the first time in her life.

"I hate you," she snarled, "I'm sorry I ever said I would go out with you."

Comments like that often attract a crowd and this time was no different.

"What's wrong?" I stammered as English students crowded around the doorway.

Diane's right index finger jabbed the air, "You know what your mother did."

She then burst into tears, turned and ran to the nurse's office in no condition to discuss the fishing trip of McMurphy, the Chief and the other mental patients.

FIVE

A group of well-read high school seniors stood around the doorway staring at me. I slipped in between a couple of them and took my seat. I hadn't done anything, yet I was overcome with a profound sense of shame. Everyone seemed to know what was going on except me. A few late-comers showed up and were immediately whispered to and then it was their turn to stare at me. I sat with my eyes locked on to my teacher, Mrs. Pratt, not daring to make eye contact with any of my former friends.

Mrs. Pratt was a nervous middle-aged woman who had been a teacher for thirty years without losing any of her nervousness. She had been my teacher freshman year and was now again my junior year. It seemed to me that she loved literature, liked her students and would have enjoyed teaching had it not involved speaking in public. She always seemed distressed when she had to get up from the safety of her desk and stand in front of us.

Mrs. Pratt had always liked me. Since I was shy and she was shy there was an unspoken bond between us. Shy people have unspoken bonds; gregarious people have boisterous, talkative bonds. During class discussions, she often called on me but never to trip me up, always when she sensed I had something to add. She was always trying to draw me out and at least build up my confidence if she couldn't build up her own.

Her teaching style was to ask frequent questions and involve each student multiple times in each discussion. Her classroom was run more like a book club than a typical English class. Yet, that day for the first time ever she left me alone. She must have known. Someone, possibly even Diane, must have filled her in on what had happened and she thought it best to leave me be.

So I sat fixated on Mrs. Pratt and wondered what it was that everyone else knew that I didn't. What had my mother done? I had only told her about my upcoming date with Diane the night before. In just a few hours, my mother had heard something she didn't like and put a stop to it, but how?

Very quickly, I became angry at myself. Whatever it was, it was my fault. Why did I tell my parents I had a date? I was bragging that's why. I had asked a girl out and she said "yes" and I was bragging about it. It was my way of saying to my mother, "I'm independent, I can make my own decisions." I should have known better.

I vaguely recall someone nearby talking about Nurse Ratched as I sat in a semi-vegetative state. My thoughts drifted to Diane. She wasn't given to emotional outbursts. She had what an old woman would describe as "a sweet disposition." I can remember vividly her crying during passages of "The Diary of Anne Frank" and her indignation at the treatment of Will Robinson in "To Kill a Mockingbird," but these were normal reactions. That morning, she was borderline hysterical. Her hatred towards me was sudden and unrestrained. Maybe my mother was right. "What do we really know about this girl?"

When the class ended and I started for the door, Mrs. Pratt gave me a sympathetic look with her top teeth biting down on her lower lip and her eyebrows raised in a non-threatening manner. There were murmurings in the hallway, something about Diane's house. During my next three classes, more eyes were on me than on the teachers and I still didn't know why. A terrible thought gripped me. "Did my mother burn Diane's house down?" My whole body clenched in panic.

By lunch time, I couldn't bear my ignorance any longer. While my classmates headed to the cafeteria, I slipped off campus. I ran at a good clip for three blocks then nearly collapsed. "Holy shit", I thought, "I am in terrible shape." I walked quickly, my fear propelling me the rest of the way. I hadn't been to Diane's house before but I had a general idea where it was. I knew the street name and the street it was off of but not the house number. When I turned the corner onto her street, there was no smell of smoke or evidence of a fire. Some police cars were up ahead but no fire trucks. My fear subsided. Slightly.

When I got close, I was able to identify Diane's house. It was the one with police tape around the yard. My fear returned in full force. The house was sheathed in white aluminum siding with the word "Slut" spray-painted in giant red letters several times along the front and the side. Four or five windows were broken and the lawn furniture was overturned.

One police officer, a body builder-type, was next door talking to a neighbor. Another cop, an older guy, stood in the driveway consoling a distraught woman I correctly assumed was Diane's mother. Trance-like, I moved towards her. The body-builder cop spotted me and cut off my advance. I yelled "I am so sorry" over him. Diane's mother didn't respond but he did.

"Son," he asked, "do you know anything about this?"

SIX

I met my first actual girlfriend early second semester sophomore year. My roommate Todd was on the football team and he would drag me to parties with him when he didn't feel like walking across campus by himself. It was at one of these when a woman even drunker than me started kissing me on the dance floor. A few minutes later, she got her roommate out of her room and me into her bed.

I had never really kissed a girl before. As you might imagine, the incident with the spray paint back home scared away any prospective candidates. Now, I was suddenly going from zero to sixty in three point eight seconds. She had enough knowledge for both of us and before long, she guided my drunk, nervous penis inside her. My thoughts ranged from, "Oh, my God, I'm having sex" to "I'm actually having sex" to "I'm finally having sex" to "Hey, I just had sex." Shortly there afterwards, she fell asleep/passed out.

For a few minutes, I lay next to her unsure of what to do next. I didn't know the proper etiquette. Should I just leave or is that rude? I'd heard Todd talk of buying a woman breakfast the next day, is that part of the deal? Should I leave some sort of a "thank you" note? I decided just to go.

I put my pants and shoes back on, never having removed my shirt. As I tiptoed toward the door, I heard the sound of crying coming from the bathroom. I gently pushed open the door to find her roommate seated on the lid of the toilet in her pajamas with her hands on her face sobbing uncontrollably.

"What's wrong?" I asked.

"Every guy likes her. She's not even nice and she leaves her dishes in the sink."

"It'll be okay," I said for no apparent reason.

"No offense but she does this every weekend. She'll pick up a random guy and bring him home. She has sex with every guy she wants. Why doesn't anybody want to fuck me? I'm much nicer than she is."

At this point, the tears came back stronger than before.

"It's just because she's pretty," she went on.

"Don't cry" I pleaded, "Don't cry."

I began kissing her tears away and before long we were having sex on the closed lid of the toilet.

In all honesty, her roommate was pretty and she wasn't. Her face was puffy and her teeth yellow and uneven. Two largish but flaccid breasts rested atop an ample belly, all supported by short, stubby legs. The sex took longer than the first time but with similar results. I told her my name was Rory, found out hers was Karen, and said good-bye.

An hour earlier, I had been an absolute virgin and now I had had sex with two women. I drunkenly laughed to myself on the way home, thought about telling my roommate Todd and then decided against it.

The following week while my roommates were at a basketball game there was a knock on the door. Karen was back with a small mousy woman at her side.

"This is Alice," Karen said and then she turned and walked away.

I was confused.

"What can I do for you, Alice?"

"Karen said you could help me," then she leaned forward and whispered, "I'm a virgin and I brought a condom."

"Alice, I don't think that's a good idea. We don't even know each other."

"You didn't know Karen either."

"I was drunk, she was crying."

"It's because I'm half black, isn't it?"

"What? No."

In all honesty, I didn't know she was half black. She looked Hispanic or Middle-Eastern. Nothing is more unnerving than being called a racist.

"All right, all right," I said and led her to the bedroom.

Over the next few weeks, I deflowered seven more of Karen's virgins. None pretty, in fact, the last one could be described as "morbidly obese." When I tried to say no, they pleaded and whined and pitched tantrums until I finally gave in. I didn't even really know what I was doing and they had no idea. There was no changing of positions, no thought of stimulating them. I was the one-eyed man in the land of the blind.

One afternoon, after the eighth (or was it the ninth?) one left, my roommate Todd suddenly entered the room and sat down on his bed. "What's going on?" he asked. "Nothing," I replied, peeking over my economics textbook.

"I don't think that's true," he said. "I think there's a lot going on. I think you're having sex with one bowser after another."

At this point, I feel compelled to tell you that I'm not a bad looking guy. Not that I'm an underwear model or anything. I have no muscle tone or any desire to work out and I have a two and a half inch long scar under my eye from a childhood incident but I have shaggy blonde hair and girls have always told me I'm cute. If not for my mother and her can of spray-paint I might have done all right in high school.

"Why are you doing this?" he demanded.

"They ask me to." I said weakly.

Eventually, he stopped laughing.

"I'm sure they do. Look, we've all made some bad choices while drunk but you're doing this sober, in the middle of the day with some of the ugliest girls on campus."

"How do you know?"

"It's not that big a school." I nodded.

I promised Todd I would stop and begged him not to tell our two other roommates. He agreed but suspected they already knew.

The next day, I remembered my mother's birthday as I finished my morning classes and headed back to my dorm for lunch. I planned to call her and then study for my American History mid-term but Karen was waiting for me. She was with another one, a bony woman with pointy nose and large eyes that hung from their sockets like overly ripe fruit.

I asked to speak to Karen privately.

"We have to stop," I said. "It's not right."

"Okay," she said, "Last one."

"No, this is ridiculous."

"I brought her all the way over here. I promise no more after this."

We argued for a few more minutes until I finally gave in.

"You have to promise me this is the last time."

"Okay, fine," she reluctantly agreed.

I got Karen's friend out of there as soon as I could then found sanctuary in the library before my roommates returned. After that came my mother's suicide, my train ride home and my father and I accidentally missing the funeral. When Mary-Ann called to tell me she was pregnant, I did what I could to calm her down. I told her I'd be back on campus in a couple of days and she and I would sort everything out. Then I hung up and wondered to myself, "Which one was Mary-Ann?"

SEVEN

When I got back to school, I called Mary Ann and we agreed to meet at what is known on campus as "The Colonel", the statue of school founder Colonel Philbin clinging heroically to "Old Nat." After the war, finding himself viewed by his fellow Southerners as a constant reminder of the battle that signaled the end of their fledgling nation, Philbin moved to Pennsylvania to be closer to his hand.

In fact, to this day, our nickname is "The Rebels" which is unusual for a school north of the Mason-Dixon Line. Students from rival schools often like to point out that there weren't any rebels in Pennsylvania. Of course, there weren't any Lions or Crusaders or Vikings in rural Pennsylvania either and that didn't stop them from using those names. Besides, there were plenty of rebels in Pennsylvania many of them are still buried in Gettysburg.

Forceful at times, charming when necessary, Philbin exacted his revenge on the North by becoming a titan in the textile industry. He died childless and widowed and bequeathed his considerable fortune to a new college with the stipulation that it be exclusively for white males. The trustees honored his request until integrating in 1929 and then during World War II, woefully short of men, defied the Colonel again, becoming coed. I suddenly wished they hadn't.

I arrived early, anxious to end the suspense of which one was Mary Ann. "Please don't be the morbidly obese one," I thought to myself. Professor Jelinak, my psych teacher, spotted me and made a beeline to offer his earnest condolences over my mother's passing. He told me not to "sweat the semester," and he'd be available during his office hours if I needed to talk. I told him her death was a shock and described the funeral as though I had been there.

I had been to enough funerals to give credible details. In fact, there was a period of about two and half years when my family went through a "funeral phase," beginning with the death of my maternal grandmother.

I never cared for the woman. She was the type who didn't like small children and liked them less when they got older. She babysat for me once when I was six. My parents were going to a Christmas party. It was remarkable that they were invited to a Christmas party and even more remarkable that they accepted.

When my grandmother arrived at the house, my father gave her strict instructions: dinner at six to six-thirty, bath over at seven, in bed at eight. As soon as they left, she put something in my milk (Benadryl I'm guessing) and I fell asleep right away. I woke up around ten and played on the living room floor with my grandmother asleep nearby until my parents arrived home.

Though my grandmother was a chain-smoking, disease-ridden woman, her death inexplicably caught my mother off-guard. For months afterwards, the surly woman's death would cause my mother to suddenly burst into tears at a moments' notice. Sometimes in the middle of the night, she would wake up crying, turn on all the lights and gather us in the living room to pray for her mother's soul.

"There is nothing worse than losing your mother," she would say. "It's your first love," and my father would nod in agreement. "You don't know what it's like to lose your mother," she often said to me. "Even Jesus didn't have to watch his mother die."

We were not a religious family. Nominally Catholic, we never went to church, not even on Christmas and Easter. Prior to her mother's death, the only time my mother ever mentioned Jesus was when she stubbed her toe or burned herself taking something out of the oven.

My mother began finding solace in baking pies for other families in our town who lost a mother or a wife. She would scan the obituaries every morning and when finding a dead local woman would set about baking some type of fruit pie. The next day, she would keep me home from school so the two of us could attend the funeral of a complete stranger.

I caught Father Barrett's act a few times. (Maybe the funeral masses were all at nine, now that I think about it) In any event, there was little variation. Each congregation received basically the same message, that the person who had passed on was happier now. One packed house, there for a young mother who had suddenly drowned leaving three small children, seemed especially unpersuaded.

We went to one mass in Polish and two in French. I was scolded once in a synagogue in the next town over for twirling my yarmulke on my finger during a reading from the Torah. At each service, we would sit in the back and my mother would cry openly though neither of us ever spoke to any of members of the grieving families.

Sometime in the following days, she would have me deliver the pies anonymously.

"They must never know it's from us," she would say. "Any deed done openly is asking for praise. Good deeds must be done in private to be sincere."

That's true," my father would murmur.

To maintain anonymity, I would deliver the pies while the family was not home.

"Imagine their delight coming home and finding a freshly baked pie in the refrigerator," my mother would muse cheerfully.

Living in a small town in the early '70's many people left their doors unlocked. My mother and I would sit in our car down the street and wait for the family to leave home, usually for church on Sunday morning. I would slip into their house, leave the pie in the refrigerator and sneak back out. Sometimes the refrigerator would be full and I would have to remove certain items and place them on the counter to make room. Twice, I returned to the car, pie in hand after finding a locked door. On both occasions, my mother found a partially opened window, pushed it further open and boosted me through.

Our secret pie operation came to an end with the death of Helen McGinn, an elderly woman who had been taking care of her equally elderly and, unbeknownst to us, blind husband Charles McGinn. We had driven by the house a few times during the day unsure if it was occupied. Finally, seeing no lights on in the early evening, my mother dispatched me from the car. Finding the front door open, I tentatively entered the house. It was twilight and I could make out the silhouettes of Hummel figurines on the mantle. I moved quickly down a dark hallway into the kitchen and flicked on the light. At that precise moment, Blind Charles McGinn bashed me in the face with a baseball bat. For a few seconds, I sat in a puddle of blood and pie.

"Get the hell out of my house," the blind man snarled.

I obliged.

My mother and I returned from the hospital that night after I received twenty two stitches.

"I think we've done enough good deeds," my father said and my mother agreed.

She never baked a pie again and her revenge on the blind man began soon afterwards and continued 'til his death and a little beyond. I touched the scar under my eye, preoccupied with these memories. "Sorry I'm late," Mary Ann said as I turned towards her.

EIGHT

"Who was that on the phone?" my father asked.

"My girlfriend." "I didn't know you had a girlfriend."

I started to cry and couldn't stop. "Oh," my father said and he got up and quickly left the room. He came back a few minutes later when I was finishing up.

He sat back down at the kitchen table.

"I suppose it's normal to cry after losing your mother," he said.

I nodded. "She was your first love."

Eventually, I broke the silence.

"Can I ask you something?...why did you...fall in love with Mom?"

He paused and I wondered if he would answer the question. He got up and filled the kettle with water and turned on the gas. "I'm going to make some tea, do you want some?" "No, thanks."

You'll have to excuse my father and me. We'd never had what you would call a real conversation. All of our prior conversations were matters of logistics, a simple relaying of information. "I'll be home at such and such time" or "We're having blah blah blah for dinner." There were never any exchanges of ideas or sharing of personal feelings, no revelations into each other's psyche or soul. Neither of us had any idea of the other's innermost thoughts. Now that my mother was gone we were attempting to for the very first time and neither of us was very good at it.

There were a few minutes of selecting the right flavor tea, then finding a tea cup and a spoon. After he settled back down he said, "I loved your mother for a lot of reasons. She was so beautiful." My father was blind in one eye. He had been half-blinded by shrapnel on Okinawa. My mother hated the Japanese long after my father had forgiven them. My mother may have been beautiful but I feel an obligation to present all the facts.

"Most people only care about what other people think," he argued, "Your mother wasn't like that. She only cared what she thought. If she thought she was right that was all that mattered."

My father impressed me at that moment. What he was saying had never occurred to me before and I have to admit it was true. It's rare when someone can provide insight into a person you've known all your life.

"I had been engaged to someone else."

I did my best to maintain a poker face for this was a bombshell.

"Right after I got drafted, just before I shipped out I got engaged to a local girl."

It was difficult for me to picture my father with another woman and I didn't try too hard. "She wrote me all the time and we were going to get married when I got back from the war. Of course, that was before I lost one of my peepers."

He gestured towards his bad eye.

"In '46 when they shipped me home from Okinawa this whole side of my face was bandaged up and I guess I scared her off."

"What a bitch!" I thought. I even like my mother more than this woman.

My Dad went to sip his tea but it was still too hot.

"It took a little while for my face to heal and when it did I didn't have another girl until I met your mother."

We both sat thinking for a moment, two disfigured Collins men lamenting their sorry history with women.

His face brightened, "Then in the spring of '59, I met your mother. She was so captivating."

He started for his tea again and then stopped.

"She was working at a women's clothing store during the day and working as a waitress at night and going to school at the same time. She was so young and she was so alive. I'd seen so much death and she was so alive."

It must have been a long, lonely thirteen years in between girl-friends and I suppose my father was willing to overlook certain short-comings like a complete lack of empathy.

We sat quietly as I tried to figure out how to phrase my next question. I wanted to ask, "Didn't you know she was nuts?" or "When did you discover she was mentally unstable?" or "You must have known something was wrong, you're not a dumb guy, why didn't you run away when you had the chance?" These are tough questions to ask a guy about his newly dead wife.

Instead, I asked, "What made her so different from everyone else?"

His tea was cool enough now and he sipped a bit.

"Your mother had a hard life. Her father killed himself, you know."

I did. In a family full of secrets this is one that had somehow escaped.

"I never told you why he did it or how," he burped and hit himself in the chest, "Excuse me" he said. "Just after your mother turned eleven your grandmother was in the hospital…pneumonia. They used to keep you there in the old days. Your grandfather got drunk and woke up your mother and her brother George in the middle of the night. He pointed a shotgun at them and then put it in his own mouth and pulled the trigger."

He took out a handkerchief and cleaned his glasses.

"After that, your mother never slept through the night again. Every night, she'd wake up suddenly as if she was expecting someone to kill themselves in front of her. That image of her father haunted her day and night."

He paused to let me take this in.

"If that weren't bad enough, your Uncle George killed himself when he was twenty-one. On the same day, his father did."

This was news to me.

"Mom said he died of tuberculosis."

My father shook his head, "No." "Suicide," he said, "It was just a few months after your mother and I married. That's why you never met him."

A chill ran through me.

"But your mother soldiered on. She was the first member in her family to graduate from college. It took six years but she made it, working two jobs. She was waitressing when I met her and I think what drew her to me was that little dog."

My father chuckled and got up and poured himself some more tea, "Are you sure you don't want any?"

The little dog story was one I'd heard many times. Here it is: my father ran over a dog and killed it. It's not a great story. He hadn't done it on purpose, of course. The dog came from the opposite direction of his good eye. In those days, Ray Charles could get a driver's license. It was a scrawny little thing with no collar and no discernible family. My father was so racked with guilt he never drove again.

"What if it had been a child?" he'd often say.

"I think when she heard that story she decided I was the one," he sat back down. "She knew I could never kill anyone or anything again."

I had never put those pieces together before. My mother had married my father because he was so unlike her Dad. She wanted a man who wouldn't threaten to murder her, someone who wouldn't murder himself or anyone else.

I had no more questions. The defense now rested after successfully presenting its insanity plea. This new information was quite illuminating.

"So," he asked, "What's your girlfriend like?"

I shrugged, "Pregnant."

NINE

I turned to face Mary-Ann. She wasn't the morbidly obese one. She was the fourth or fifth one. She was fairly tall and skinny. "Gangly" was the word that flashed in my head. She had a recessive chin and one of her eyes seemed to have a mind of its own. We had had sober sex in the middle of the afternoon just a few weeks ago and yet her face was only vaguely familiar.

"I'm Rory," I said unnecessarily.

We shook hands like two business associates meeting for the first time. We each took a breath.

"I have some questions for you," she said, "Let's sit over here."

We sat side by side under the hindquarters of Philbin's horse Old Nat, my hideous scar facing her funky eye.

In real life, Old Nat was, of course, a stallion. The immortalized granite version is a mare. One can imagine the conversation with the sculptor commissioned for the job in the early 1920's. "We would like a realistic sculpture of Colonel Philbin atop his trusted horse with one hoof raised signifying the battle wounds suffered by his master, muscles should be taut, head turned projecting an intense kinetic energy but no, horse dick, I repeat, no horse dick."

She took out a small notebook and a pen. She flipped it open to a series of questions. Underneath each question, she had left room to write the answer.

"Where are you from?"

"You're taking notes?"

"I think we should learn as much about each other as possible."

She held the pen and pad in the ready position awaiting my answer.

"Addison," I said, "it's a little town about sixty miles from here. How 'bout you?" "Tilden, Ohio." I made a mental note.

She wrote down "Addison, Pennsylvania" in neat cursive writing. I had never been interviewed before and I wasn't sure if I liked the feeling. It wasn't so much that I didn't like talking about myself I just had no experience. I had never been asked more than one or two questions at one time and I felt unworthy to be the subject of a biography.

When she asked me, "As a child, what did you dream of growing up to be?" I had no answer. I wasn't like other kids. I didn't dream of being a football player or an astronaut or a rock star or the President of the United States. I just wanted to get the fuck out of my house. I wanted to live a life that was "normal." I didn't know if there was such a thing as "normal" but I knew it wasn't what was going on inside 68 Spring View Lane.

"I don't remember," I lied.

She wrote this down.

"I've always dreamed of being a mother," she replied ominously.

"Do you have any siblings?" I shook my head "no" prompting a near gasp.

"A singleton," she muttered.

I've been an only child my whole life and I had never heard that term before.

"A singleton?"

"I'm a sociology major. It's important you know that about me. Did you know that singletons suffer from depression at a much higher rate than people with siblings?"

I didn't but I was starting to see why. "It's because they lack an emotional support group. I think we should have a big family."

My mouth opened and closed and nothing came out.

"What religion are you?" I hesitated.

"I'm Catholic" she said.

"Me, too" I said, which was technically true and seemed to make her happier than any of my previous answers. Like everyone else, she was surprised I was Polish and not Irish. Her Mom was Hungarian and her Dad was something I can't remember.

She flipped a page in her notebook. The questions arrived one after another seemingly without end. My father's profession did my mother work, favorite movie, favorite book, favorite play, favorite sport, favorite color (who over the age of seven has a favorite color?) "Mine's blue," she revealed with gravitas. We rotated our seats along Philbin's back chasing an anemic sun. "She has to be getting cold," I thought, "she's as skinny as I am."

As the interview continued, a certain rhythm developed. It began with a probing question followed by my answer followed by precise notes followed by thoughtful answers to her own questions all building to the inevitable climax. It all came down to the big question, Final Jeopardy, the whole reason we'd spent the last ninety minutes leaning against the replica of a dead horse.

"When do you want to get married?"

Gently, but firmly, I said, "Mary Ann, I don't think we should get married." Tears began welling up in her rogue eye.

"I'm Catholic," she said, "I can't have an abortion and I can't be an unwed mother," she said. "Children of unwed mothers are two and a half times more likely to end up in prison." "But we hardly know each other."

"That's what this was for" she declared, waving, Exhibit A, the notebook.

This wasn't going the way I thought it would.

"You'll love me, I know you will. I'm smart and I'm nice and I get good grades."

She stood over me now.

"I love children. I've babysat since I was twelve."

"I just think-"

"Don't you see? My mother got married when she was nineteen."

I didn't see.

She looked around to make sure no one was listening.

"I've only had…" she muffled the word "sex" "one time in my life and it was with you. It was meant to be. It's a miracle."

Major Philbin's men were ill-prepared for the Battle of Gettysburg. Exhausted from long, sweltering days of marching in worn boots either too small or too large with bellies bloated and gaseous from eating too many peaches, they pressed on. With Philbin on horseback, shouting encouragement, prayers and threats, they stood tall as the well-fed boys from Minnesota bore down on them. Their little battle within the big battle raged on inconclusively until Philbin, clutching his horse's reins, had his left hand blown clean off by a smoothbore musket ball. He withstood the pain, temporarily, even directing a gap in the line to be closed before losing consciousness from the loss of blood.

Three days later, Major, soon to be Colonel Philbin, came to with other wounded men, moaning and swearing, on the back of a horse drawn cart rumbling for the Virginia border. He had lost his hand and the South had lost its chance of conquering the North.

I only mention it because I was facing a similarly unrelenting onslaught.

"You wouldn't use me, would you? You're too nice a guy and we have so much in common. We're soul mates, please."

There was no let up to the barrage of tears and accusations. "Jesus," I thought.

"Okay, okay," I said, "I'll marry you."

TEN

"Who's going to love him now?" my mother screamed, "He'll die alone."

My parents didn't fight often enough for my taste but in those rare instances when my father stood up to my mother it was always behind their closed bedroom door and I could only ever hear her side of the argument so my father's response to her, "That old man ruined his beautiful face," has been lost to history.

My mother possessed a medley of battlefield tactics. Initially, she might yell and scream. If this failed to produce the desired results, she might sob uncontrollably and look hurt. If victory still eluded her, she would withdraw completely and become sullen and distant. Philbin, a master strategist, would have admired her adaptability and tenacity.

My father, on the other hand, only had one approach, remain calm and hope that the simple truth of your argument will carry the day. He was like an early model of a World War I army tank. He would press on straight ahead at the exact same speed with no feints and no diversions.

This was the fight my mother and father had the night I returned from the hospital with twenty-two stitches under my eye. On the drive home, my mother cried hysterically the whole way. Every time she looked over at me, she would re-erupt in a fit of despair. At eleven years old, I found myself, freshly wounded and still dazed, consoling her.

"It'll be okay, Mom," I said over and over.

For months after blind Charles McGinn used my face for batting practice, my mother made me wear a large bandage under my eye.

She continued to do so even after the doctor proclaimed me "healed." She would remove the bandage at night and put on a fresh one in the morning, sometimes closing her eyes to avoid seeing it.

When the bandage finally came off for good, it was hard for her to look at me without bursting into tears. If I was with my mother at the market or at a clothing store and an old lady commented in typical old lady fashion, "What a handsome boy," my mother would say, "He used to be." Even years later, any innocuous question I had for her like, "What time is Dad coming home?" or "What's for dinner?" might be met with a scowl followed by a "that damn scar."

I learned how to minimize my scar as I ventured out into the world. If there was a cute girl in my class I would make sure to sit on her right and relinquish only my profile. When forced to engage in direct conversation, even with a man, I would become interested in something to my right and look off in the distance with my head turned while we spoke. In the summertime, I wore oversized sunglasses that didn't quite cover it but at least stole focus. In the winter, while sledding or having snowball fights, I'd wear a ski mask even in milder weather.

I became an expert in noticing other people's defects. I could spot a missing tooth, a mole or a port wine stain from five hundred yards. Upon meeting someone, I would instantly begin searching for a limp, a receding hairline or facial features either too big or too small. I found comfort in knowing that others were similarly punished by God and cultivated a circle of equally misshapen friends.

I don't know about you but I honestly harbored no resentment towards Mr. McGinn. He didn't know it was me he was bashing before, during or even after he hit me. We were complete strangers except for that one brief interaction. He was blind and assumed I was an intruder in his home. How was he to know I had come bearing pie?

My mother, of course, was not one to let things slide. She would have her revenge even against the elderly, even against the blind. Two weeks after my accident, I came home from school to find her in the backyard with a crowbar. When she found the crowbar insufficient, she purchased a small tool I never learned the name of but was similar to a chisel.

Every day, on the back stairs while my father was at work, she would use the chisel-like instrument to clear some room around a nail on the backstairs. She would then place the V of the crowbar around the nail and lift it out of the plank. She practiced lifting each nail out of its home and then replacing it before my father would come home.

After a week, she needed my help.

"Stand over there," she'd say and I would have to stand to the side of the house. "Tell me if you hear anything."

While I leaned against the house, staring at nothing in particular, she would quietly chisel around the nail and then gently crowbar it from the staircase. She would do this on both sides until the planks were removed.

"Did you hear anything?" she asked.

When I told her I didn't she smiled and said, "I'm ready."

Very late that night, from what I could piece together later, she drove to somewhere near Mr. McGinn's house. Using her stealthy crowbar and chisel-like thing she successfully removed the top two rows of planks on Mr. McGinn's staircase while the old man slept.

You can imagine the results as the next morning, the 83-year-old blind man, clutching his white cane, left the house for his early morning trip to the coffee shop and stepped out unsuspectingly onto stairs that were no longer there.

"He nearly broke his neck," Chief of Police Harrington was quoted as saying after McGinn sustained multiple fractures.

"Who Would Do Such a Thing?" queried the front page of the Addison Sentinel the following day. Teenage pranksters seemed to be the best guess.

Three weeks later, the local evening news mentioned the incident during their story on the rise of teenage delinquency much to the delight of my mother. She smiled at me as I set the table.

"Nobody ruins my boy's beautiful face and gets away with it," she mused with a lilt in her voice.

ELEVEN

Three weeks after my marriage proposal at Philbin's horse, Karen knocked urgently on Mary Ann's bedroom door.

"Rory?" she asked, "Are you in there?"

I was still half asleep.

"I think you're going to want to see this."

Now that Mary Ann had met and decided to spend the rest of our lives together, I'd been sleeping in her room every night at her insistence. We had sex whenever her roommate wasn't around including one time with me on the bottom and Mary Ann on top. The downside was that Philbin College only provided single beds which made things very cramped for betrothed sophomores. We would lay, side by side, two heads on one pillow, jostling for space eight hours at a time. Sometimes I would sneak back to my dorm for an afternoon nap.

News of our pregnancy and subsequent engagement had made the two of us instant campus celebrities. I was constantly either being congratulated or looked at with disdain, often by total strangers. On those rare occasions when I returned to my dorm room for sleep or replenish my wardrobe, my roommates Dale and Kevin would instantly stop talking and exchange amused looks.

Todd seemed to especially enjoy my return visits. He would shut off the TV in the living room, follow me to the bedroom and sit at his desk and watch me pack.

"It's a shame you missed health class in high school," he said, "It was the one class where I learned something. It seems scientists have invented something you can put on your cock and it keeps women from getting pregnant."

"Now you tell me," I mumbled.

As Karen again knocked on the door and called my name, I regained consciousness. "One second," I replied, throwing on some jeans. Mary Ann, in her flannel pajamas, sat up, "Come in."

Warily, Karen poked her head in and then the rest of her body followed.

"Something bad has happened," she said looking my way, "Concerning you."

"What is it?" asked Mary Ann on my behalf.

"It's better if you come and take a look for yourselves."

It took me a moment to put on socks and shoes. Mary Ann donned a robe and slippers and we followed Karen down two flights of stairs to the common room.

"It's right here," Karen said, pointing to the dorm bulletin board that contained such items as "Guitar for Sale" and "Need a ride?" The one that caught my eye was dead center. In bold letters it read, "Rory Collins is the father of my baby, too, Irene Lawson." Mary Ann and I froze. Karen looked grim, "She put a copy of this in every dorm on campus."

"Who is Irene Lawson?" I asked. Karen puffed out her cheeks providing a non-verbal description. "Good lord" I thought, "It's the morbidly obese one." Mary Ann began to cry, scowling at me with both her good and bad eye. "It was before we met," I mumbled, not entirely truthfully.

Karen ripped the notice down and crumpled it up.

"I think she's full of shit," she said. "It's a bunch of bullshit from a fat, fuckin' liar. There is no way she's pregnant and her Dad was never a croupier at Monte Carlo."

Neither Mary Ann nor I had any idea how to respond to that.

"I think we should settle this right now," Karen went on. "She lives in 523 in this dorm."

She was like a field commander ready to lead her troops into battle.

"Okay," I said eager to do my duty.

I turned to kiss Mary Ann good-bye.

"Don't you touch me," she screamed, drawing considerable attention.

In the elevator, Karen informed me that Irene was roommates with Alice, the half-black one who gave me the choice of sex or racism. I winced. Karen was right about Irene's roommate but slightly wrong about the room. We discovered Irene actually lived in 532, not 523, after waking up a less than mellow stoner.

When we knocked on 532, Alice opened the door.

"Oh, it's you," she said upon seeing me. She half-heartedly said "Hi" to Karen.

"Is Irene here?" I asked.

Alice shook her head, "No."

"She told me what you did to her."

What I did to her? Give me a break, none of this was my idea. I was doing these women a favor. Besides, if Alice hadn't blabbed to Irene what we did, Irene wouldn't have showed up insisting on her turn.

"I'll tell her you came by."

"Do you know where she is?" Karen asked.

"She works at the bakery in town on Saturday mornings."

"The bakery," Karen scoffed, "Quel surprise."

Alice semi-slammed the door in our faces. Thanks a lot, Alice. That's the last time I help you lose your virginity.

We headed back to the elevator.

"I can give you a ride to the bakery," said Karen, "But I have to be at work at the supermarket by ten so you'll have to walk home."

I nodded.

On the way, Karen filled me in on some of Irene's other fabrications. Aside from lying about her father being a croupier, Irene would send herself flowers on Valentine's Day. She told stories of romantic weekends in Paris with imaginary boyfriends. She spoke of various movie stars as being family friends who regularly attended parties at her parents' home. How this happened in Waterville, Maine was anyone's guess.

When we got to the bakery it was crowded and Irene pretended not to see us as she waited on customers. We took a number. After several minutes, it was finally our turn. "Can I help you?" Irene asked without a hint of recognition. Karen, elbows on the counter, leaned forward and hissed, "You're not pregnant, your Dad isn't a croupier and I bet you've never even been to Paris."

Irene's eyes narrowed, "I have so. I've been to the top of the Eiffel Tower."

We seemed to be getting off topic and the man behind us huffed impatiently. I nudged Karen. "You're not pregnant. You know you're not. You're making it up and you're messing things up between Rory and Mary Ann."

Irene pursed her lips.

"I am so pregnant," she bellowed, "With his baby. You are going to hear from my lawyer."

TWELVE

After Irene threatened me with her lawyer I didn't know what to say. Karen and I just stood there while Irene helped the man behind us pick out six bagels, two sesame, two cinnamon raisin and two plain. Eventually, the manager came over and kicked us out. God bless him.

Out on the sidewalk, Karen checked her watch. "I have to get to the supermarket. My boss is an asshole when I'm late."

"What do I do when her lawyer calls me?"

"She doesn't have a lawyer. She's a sophomore in college who works part-time at a bakery." She checked her watch again.

"I really have to go."

She started to move towards her car.

"Why did you do this to me?"

She stopped and turned. "Do what to you? What, I made you have sex with other women? Are you shitting me? You loved it."

She was pretty angry so I didn't push it. "You seemed pretty happy with Mary Ann the past few weeks."

I just stood there.

"Look, Irene is a pathological liar. I wouldn't be surprised if her real name isn't Irene. She's not pregnant. This is all going to blow over in a couple of days."

Karen got into her car and drove off.

I had a long walk back to my dorm room to think about what she said. She was right of course. I did like it. Not so much the sex but I liked feeling loveable. More importantly, I liked feeling significant for the first time in my life.

When I got back to my dorm, I ate some cereal while Todd stood over me.

"A little bird tells me that you've knocked up another one."

I cut up a banana.

"Are you going to marry this one, too?"

"I don't think this one is really pregnant," I said, "She's a pathological liar."

Todd blew air from his lips.

"I don't know" he said, shaking his head from side to side, "She could keep up that lie for quite some time. No one could tell if she were showing or not. Do you want me to get an elephant gun and put her out of her misery?"

I finished my cereal.

I didn't leave my dorm room the rest of the weekend. A couple of times the phone rang and I jumped in anticipation of a call from Irene's lawyer. On Monday, I ventured out to go to class. Everywhere I went I was whispered about and shunned and met with dirty looks. It was the Diane incident all over again with one big difference. When that had occurred some people were smart enough to realize I wasn't the perpetrator. My mother was regarded as the town kook and a certain cross section felt sorry for me. No one said anything of course but I could see it in their eyes.

There were women who had supported me during my engagement to Mary Ann, women who found something noble about my willingness to accept responsibility but now I lost that fan base. The men across campus, who were never on my side, now found me to be some sort of freak. Only Todd would speak to me and that's only if you count lobbing fat jokes at me as speaking. "I bought a baby crib for your new girlfriend. I'm having it reinforced with steel girders."

On Tuesday, on my way out of Psych on my way to Am Lit, I heard someone yell my name. I turned to see Karen running towards me in the middle of the busy quad. She was grinning broadly, "I've got proof. I've got proof she's not pregnant."

She was waving something in her hand.

"Look," she said, holding up a bloody tampon triumphantly, "This is hers."

The momentary surge of joy receded immediately in an undertow of shame. Heads snapped my way. Someone burst out with a laugh.

"Mind your own business," Karen snarled.

Quietly, still clutching her trophy, Karen continued, "I followed Irene into the lady's room. I peeked out from the stalls and saw her put this into the receptacle. She couldn't deny it was hers. She said she was sorry."

I nodded, "Thanks for doing that. I'm just glad it's over."

"Me, too" she smiled. "Here. You better give this to Mary Ann."

THIRTEEN

"What do you think about names?" Mary Ann asked, her chin resting in the middle of my back as my body teetered over the edge of her bed.

"I think people should have them."

Silence.

"What do you mean?"

"It was just a joke."

She looked at me blankly but then continued, "There is something living inside me. Isn't that amazing? Inside my body there's a living thing."

I wanted to say, "A bug flew into my mouth once" but after the way my name joke went over I decided to stay quiet.

"I'm having a craving," she said while putting her jeans on. She was as skinny as ever. "I'm having a craving for waffles. A lot of pregnant women get cravings you know. I was reading about it in here."

She got down on her knees and retrieved a box from under her bed. She opened it and pulled out, "What to Expect When You're Expecting." She clutched it to her chest as if someone wanted to take it from her.

"I had to go into town to get it. They didn't have it at the school bookstore."

She sat at the foot of the bed flipping through it. I shut my eyes.

Moments later, she shook me, "C'mon, I have a craving for waffles. The father is supposed to understand when the mother gets a craving. We'll have to go into town. They won't have it in the cafeteria. I know just the place."

We walked into town in the rain. It was one of those March Pennsylvania days with no spring in sight when the wind blows straight from Philadelphia to Pittsburgh with nary a peep from the timid Alleganies.

We walked past the bakery where Irene works on our way to the diner. We could see Irene's ample profile as we sloshed past.

"I bet she's lying to the customers about the price of blueberry muffins."

Mary Ann let out a guttural sound which I counted as a laugh.

We grabbed the last two stools at the diner. We were the only two college students. The rest of the patrons gave the impression of being regulars. Joyless conversation filtered from one booth to the next and from one end of the diner to the other. We were like party crashers at an event no one cared to attend but had no other place to go.

Millwood was made up of college students and townies, with very little interaction. The two camps weren't enemies exactly though each group maintained an implied disdain. They were like two incompatible species placed by an indifferent zookeeper in the same cage, each group having no use for the other.

Eventually, the waitress came our way.

"I'll have the scrambled eggs," said Mary Ann.

Scrambled eggs? "I thought you had a craving for waffles?"

"I changed my mind."

"I could have made you scrambled eggs back in the room," I pointed out as water dripped from my jeans onto the floor. "Pregnant women are often irrational. The book says so."

I had the waffles.

Halfway through the meal, Mary Ann jerked her head up inspired by a sudden thought, "Do you know what nesting is? The book says it's the next phase for an expectant mother. She begins preparing her home for the baby's arrival. We could get started today fixing up the baby's room."

"We don't have a baby's room."

"We can fix my dorm room up for the baby and me."

"The baby won't be here 'til October. You'll be in a different room next fall."

"I can request the same room. Please, please, can we get start nesting today?"

Her good eye pleaded.

"Okay," I said, not exactly sure what it was I was agreeing to.

The diner seemed glad to be rid of us for as soon as we stood up, two of their kind swooped into our seats and immediately joined what passed for banter. Once outside, Mary Ann said, "The first step is wallpaper. Wallpaper will make the room feel like a nursery."

"I should probably start my Psych paper."

"You promised we could start nesting. Come on, there's a store not too far that sells home furnishings."

Despite the rain, her face took on a happy glow.

"I think a Laura Ashley décor would be nice."

"That sounds kind of girly. What if it's a boy?"

"Well, what do you suggest?"

"How 'bout Babar wallpaper?"

"Babar?"

"Yeah, you know, the French elephant."

"I know who Babar is."

I can remember being small and my mother reading the Babar stories to me. I would bring the book over to her and she would say, "Not this one again." Yet, she would give in and although I wasn't allowed to sit on her lap I would sit next to her and soak up each of the little elephant's adventures.

At some point during the first grade I learned to read. One night after dinner, to
display my amazing new skill, I brought a book with me into the kitchen.

"Go" I said, pointing at each word, "Go, Dog, Go."

My parents stared dumbstruck as if I changed water into wine.

"Would you look at that?" my father said finally.

My mother glared at him and then crouched down so she and I were eye to eye.

"I'm still going to read to you, don't you understand? They are not taking that away from me."

That night, she read to me for two solid hours nudging me awake every time I began to doze off.

A week later, during school vacation, she changed tactics.

"Look what I got you,"

She said, handing me my very own loose-leaf notebook and my first pen.

"We're going to write together."

I didn't want to write. We wrote in school. That was plenty as far as I was concerned. Nevertheless, from then on, she postponed her writing sessions until I got home from school. Then she and I would sit across from each other at the kitchen table with our notebooks and our pens. Though she would guard her notebook like the Soviet Union guarded its air space, she was free to read what I had written so I never wrote about her. At first, I just wrote random words and then simple sentences and then eventually about what had happened that day at school. Sometimes she would make me cross something out. "That's not a nice thing to say" was her typical complaint. "It's important to be kind."

After dinner, she would sit in her faded red chair and I would sit nearby on the couch. I wasn't allowed to move a muscle. If I had to go to the bathroom it would just have to wait. It was always fiction and always books that she loved: "Heidi", "Anne of Green Gables", "Little Women" to name a few.

When I reached the seventh grade I told her I was too old to have my mother read to me. She wouldn't hear of it. When I entered the ninth grade, I explained, very calmly, one night that although I've enjoyed our reading time together I simply had too much homework now that I'm in high school. My Dad nodded vigorously in agreement. We thought we had her but we didn't. She began reading my English assignments to me. Since it takes longer to talk than to read aloud our sessions doubled in length. She'd won again.

The weird thing is, it actually worked in the sense that I always got good grades in English. I didn't skim parts or blow off the assignment like some other kids. Truth be told, it was somewhat pleasant. She wasn't yelling at me or criticizing me, she was just reading and it was usually a pretty good story.

She has some rules, of course. She wouldn't say "fuck". When that word appeared in "Catcher in the Rye" or "One Flew over the Cuckoo's Nest" she would say "funk" instead. I'd have to bite my lip to keep from laughing. If there was a sex scene, she would become embarrassed and then angry and skip over it. I'd read it on my own later on.

She continued to read to me and we continued to write together until I was sixteen. Until the Diane incident. After that neither one of us wanted anything to do with the other. One morning while she was in the shower, I threw away my notebooks in a misguided attempt to hurt her. I wished I had kept them.

When I got to college I rebelled again by becoming interested in non-fiction. I became a history not an English major. I would live in the real world even if my mother chose not to. Although, I have to admit, thanks to her, I've always loved a good story.

"I think Babar would be cool."

"Our first fight," she mused, taking my arm somehow forgetting the two days she didn't speak to me when Irene pretended she was also carrying my baby.

The home furnishings store was cramped and tired waiting impatiently for a big store to come along and commit corporate euthanasia.

"What the hell is Babar?" the saleswoman barked, "This is all we got."

There was no Laura Ashley, no clowns or ducks or anything re-sembling an infant's décor. There were some flowers, one with old ships, solid and striped colors. "Let's go with the yellow one," Mary Ann suggested, "It looks like sunbeams."

I actually know how to wallpaper. My mother and I wallpapered our whole house one summer. It was the summer after she ruined my first date and the charges against her were dismissed. I had lost any desire to please her. My disdain for her was finally equal to hers for me. It was not an open hostility but a silent seething cold war be-tween two superpowers. Picture Nixon and Breshnev measuring, cut-ting and gluing wallpaper in a grudge filled vacuum with little talk and no eye contact.

This time wallpapering was actually pleasant. Mary Ann was cheerful as we moved the bed away from the wall and set to work. As each new long yellow stripe stretched from ceiling to floor she would give my arm an appreciative squeeze or give me a quick peck on the lips. When we were two-thirds done, her roommate entered and dropped her belongings. "What the fuck are you doing?"

"We're…we're getting the room ready for the baby" Mary Ann stammered.

"Jesus Christ, are you out of your mind? I'm telling Greg."

Shortly afterwards, Mary Ann's RA, Greg, a 22-year-old scruffy bearded beatnik stood at the door. He actually smacked himself in the forehead like Ricky Ricardo.

"Mary Ann," he whimpered, "Don't you see? I'm going to have to write you up for this."

While the three of them hashed things out, I headed for the safety of my dorm room. "Oh, good," Todd beamed as I entered, "Daddy's home."

He was sitting on the couch watching college basketball on TV. His belly having grown large since the football season ended.

"I've been thinking about baby names for you." He paused to belch. "If it's a boy Todd, if it's a girl Toddina."

My roommate Dale snickered in the next room.

Two days later, mid-Civil War lecture, someone tapped me on the shoulder.

"I think she wants you," he said pointing at Mary Ann in the doorway.

She was signaling me to come to her. I looked at the clock. There was still twenty more minutes left in the Battle of Appomattox. She waved her arms angrily. I put my notebook under my arm and slinked out the door.

"I've been kicked out of housing," she said on the verge of tears. "They said I could reapply in the summer but for the rest of the semester I have no place to live."

She sniffed. "You can stay with me. It'll be fine."

FOURTEEN

Mary Ann had too much stuff to keep it all at my place so Karen agreed to hold on to two of her suitcases. When we got to my dorm, Dale was on his way out and Kevin was studying. I explained Mary Ann's predicament and they seemed okay about it. It wasn't their reaction that really concerned me, it was Todd's. Especially since Todd, Mary Ann and I would be sleeping in the same room. He wasn't home.

"This bathroom is disgusting," Mary Ann decided after a quick survey of the premises. She made me clean the toilet, finding a brush under the sink that I never knew we had. I came out of the bathroom to find the bed had been made, covered with a bright yellow bedspread and adorned with three stuffed animals.

I made a couple of grilled cheese sandwiches. Halfway through our dinner, Todd entered. He stopped short upon seeing us and took a moment to take in the scene. "Todd…um…this is my girlfriend Mary Ann."

"Ah", he said with a sweeping bow, "Rory has told me so much about you."

She was momentarily delighted with his chivalry.

"If I'm not mistaken, you're the first of the pregnant ones, right?"

This was met with Mary Ann's famous scowl and we were off to a rocky start.

"Mary Ann needs to stay with us for a little while."

"Oh, really?" he burst out laughing. "Do I at least get a say in the choice of wallpaper?" Mary Ann threw her sandwich back on her plate.

"How did you know about that?" I asked.

"Oh, I follow your exploits with great interest, I assure you."

The three of us looked from one to another. It was a Mexican stand-off.

"Do you mind if she stays?"

"I have no place to go," Mary Ann added, a little too pathetically.

"Madam, I wouldn't dream of putting a pregnant woman out. I'd be happy to discuss this further but I'm on my way to take a shit. If you'll excuse me."

Todd never seemed to study. As a communications major and a football player his workload was laughable. He seemed to pride himself on getting by having done as little as possible. It was as if he considered studying to be cheating and his strict code of ethics would not abide by it. His success in his class in public speaking was his magnum opus. The way I heard it, the most important speech of the semester focused on current events. Each student was to choose a controversial topic and use examples and expert opinions to bolster their argument. When it was Todd's turn, he simply stood up and gave an impromptu pro-death penalty lecture.

"These guys are the scum of the earth," he pointed out. "Why should a guy who rapes your grandmother be allowed to live?"

His arguments were persuasive enough to warrant a B+, only his lack of the required written outline depriving him of an A.

Until Mary Ann moved in, I didn't notice how much Todd walked around in just his boxer shorts. During the winter months after football ended, his arms, chest and shoulders had grown more massive from weightlifting and his belly had doubly grown now that he was no longer running sprints.

"Do you have to walk around like that?" Mary Ann complained.

"I don't have any jammies. Besides," he reasoned, grabbing two fistfuls of his protruding stomach, you're going to look like this soon enough."

By Wednesday, a pattern had developed. Dale would eat early and go to the library and Kevin would come home late from God knows where. At seven o'clock, Mary Ann, Todd and I would have dinner together. While I made pasta, Mary Ann and Todd would sit at the table and eye each other cautiously like two boxers during a pre-fight weigh-in.

Mary Ann liked to start conversations by posing a baby-related philosophical question. "Do you think the baby will be more musically inclined or athletically inclined?" Or "Do you think the baby will grow up to be introverted like you or extroverted like me?"

I would then try and formulate some answer based on nothing, concerning a baby that was still six and a half months from being born.

When Mary Ann wondered, "What famous person should the baby try and emulate?", Todd cut her off.

"I don't want to hear about the baby."

"What?"

"You heard me. I'm not interested. It's not my kid. I don't want to hear about it."

She seethed but I was secretly delighted. Mary Ann talked about the baby twenty four hours a day. I was sick of it and it was my kid.

Todd seemed to enjoy the tension. He continued to join us whenever we ate. Mary Ann would not say a word when he entered the room. The longer the silences the happier Todd seemed. These scenes became very reminiscent of my childhood, silent, uncomfortable meals where the only sounds were of chewing or a fork hitting the plate. Mary Ann was a younger, skinnier, cyclopean version of my mother. Todd was a younger, huger, cherubic version of my father with one notable exception. Todd had balls. My father hated tension and sought to avoid it. Todd was amused by it and was happy to create more.

Each night was an adventure. Todd was reasonably well behaved in the common areas but his room was his domain. He was incredibly gaseous and at bedtime would fart loudly and proudly and seemingly at will. Mary Ann would bark, "That's disgusting" and Todd would reply in mock horror, "You hurt its feelings."

Mary Ann and I were never alone. Whereas her old roommate was always at the library, at her part-time job or at her boyfriend's Todd was always around. You never knew when he would burst through the door and you would never know what condition he'd be in. Meanwhile, I was twenty years old and sleeping in a single bed with my girlfriend. I was aroused at all times. If I had cut myself shaving, nothing would have happened since all the blood in my body was too busy flowing to my penis. My only hope was Thursday night.

Football players always had a curfew on Friday night and Saturday night there was always something happening on campus. So every Thursday, Todd headed into town to "check out the local talent," in his words.   I longed for Thursday.

Finally, it came and as soon as Todd left I pressed Mary Ann for sex.

"We can't anymore."

"What? Why not?"

"Because of the baby. Some scientists believe that memories start in the womb. I don't think my daughter's first memories should be of her father's penis."

Suddenly, I was a pervert for wanting to have sex with my girl-friend.

"I'm pretty sure her eyes are closed," I pointed out to no avail.

Instead, we went to the student union to catch the movie "Alien." Mary Ann shrieked and hid her head every time the monster appeared. How's that for Freudian symbolism? After the movie we grabbed an ice cream and when we returned to the room we found a tube sock on the door knob.

"We can't go in."

"Why not?"

"A tube sock on the door knob is the international sign of 'I'm having sex, don't come in.'"

"I've never heard that."

Even Inuits from the Canadian tundra and Maori tribesmen from the jungles of New Zealand know when they come home to find a tube sock on the igloo or hut it means "Don't come in, I'm having sex."

"I'm sure it won't be long" I said.

Mary Ann lay, eyes closed, curled up on one couch while I sat on the opposite couch watching a rerun of an old sitcom with the volume turned down. The argument began as a low rumble in the next room. Pretty soon, Todd, clearly drunk, began yelling, "This ain't no picnic" over and over. Neither Mary Ann nor I knew what he meant by this but very quickly a middle-aged woman of about thirty-five emerged from his room. Disheveled and annoyed, she exited without eye contact and slammed the door. We entered my bedroom to find Todd snoring serenely.

Three hours later, Mary Ann elbowed me awake. Todd's shadowy figure was standing over her.

"You're so pretty," he mumbled reaching out to touch her hair. She yelped and I turned on the light. Todd blinked several times but otherwise remained frozen.

"Get away from me," Mary Ann warned.

"But you're so pretty," he reiterated and reached out again.

"Get away!" she squealed pushing his shirtless belly with both hands. He teetered, blinked again, and then vomited on her head, neck and torso.

Mary Ann's screams filled the room. I scrambled out of bed and rushed her into the shower. She was convulsing now and crying like a small child.

"It's so cold, so cold" she repeated as the water engulfed her.

"It'll warm up, it'll just take a minute."

Someone was pounding on the door.

"I'll be right back."

Our R.A. Tony in a tee-shirt and sweats stood in the hall.

"What the hell's going on?"

"Todd threw up on my girlfriend."

"What?"

"Todd's drunk and he threw up on my girlfriend. She kind of freaked out."

"God damn it, she's not supposed to be sleeping here. She woke up the whole building." "You know Todd."

I returned to Mary Ann.

"It's too hot!"

I found an acceptable temperature and held her as her body shook. We soaped and shampooed fully clothed removing what I could of the stench. We spent the rest of the night on separate living room couches.

In the morning, we ate cereal quietly in the kitchen still in shock over the events of the night before. Eventually, Todd emerged dressed in a hooded sweatshirt and jeans. He and Mary Ann locked eyes momentarily.

"Sorry," he mumbled and left. Mary Ann whirled on me.

"That's it? Sorry? Why didn't you say something?"

"He said he was sorry."

"He practically raped me last night and you didn't say anything."

"He didn't come close to raping you. He just said you were pretty. It's a compliment." "And throwing up on me? What do you call that…a marriage proposal?"

"He was drunk. He obviously feels bad."

"We're getting an apartment today. I'm not staying here one more minute."

FIFTEEN

"We'd like a place with two bedrooms, maybe a patio overlooking a garden and a fireplace."

Mrs. Cribbs laughed out loud, exposing cigarette stained teeth.

"Honey", she explained, gently patting Mary Ann's hand, "On your budget, we'll be lucky to find a janitor's closet."

Millwood began as a section of the town of Hillcrest, becoming incorporated on its own after outgrowing its mother. It was originally a series of tiny wooden dwellings inhabited by Colonel Philbin's mill workers. The Confederate Colonel's first foray north of the Mason-Dixon Line resulted in defeat and a missing hand. His second produced a successful factory, millions of dollars, and, upon his demise, a college that still bears his name. The former slave owner who fought to retain his slaves made a fortune owning a factory that employed small children for eighty-five cents per day, proving once again that America is the land of opportunity.

As he aged, Philbin's stature among his former enemies grew, for by praising a vanquished foe they were raising their own stature. Late in life, Philbin co-authored an article for a national magazine about Robert E. Lee entitled, "The Greatest Man I ever knew." The article featured a long philosophical discussion on the way back to Virginia between Lee and the young Major Philbin. During the journey, according to Philbin, Lee and Philbin discussed man's violent nature and how a young man's desire for glory inevitably results in an old man's love of peace. The fact that this diatribe supposedly took place on the trip home from Gettysburg during which Philbin was freshly amputated, drugged and riding in a cart full of soldiers in a similar state must have stretched the credulity of even the most gullible sub-scribers.

Although Philbin's Textiles no longer existed, one of his factories' sites was now used as a microbrewery and the cramped brick apartments built for his employees in the twenties were still around. Mrs. Cribbs showed us three of them. Each one was a grim tiny windowed two bedroom with one of the bedrooms already occupied. We would have to share the kitchen and bathroom with a total stranger but at least we'd have a bedroom to ourselves for once.

It was as if Mary Ann and I were the bachelorette on "The Dating Game" and Mrs. Cribbs were the emcee. She would take us to each of the three apartments. We would meet the tenants and then choose which contestant was right for us. We would "win" a year in a crumby apartment, no expenses paid.

First up was a Mr. Fitzhugh. His doorbell was broken and Mrs. Cribbs knocked repeatedly until he finally came to the door. Fitzhugh was the type whose clothes conveyed one age and his body and face another. His jeans and tee-shirt looked out of place on his saggy middle-aged frame underneath a face partially hidden by a black and white speckled beard.

"Sorry," he said, "I was taking a nap."

He led us inside and up two flights of stairs. There was a faint whiff of marijuana in the air. The living room featured a Bob Dylan poster on one wall and one of the Beatles on the other. Milk crates full of record albums reached the ceiling. The bathroom door was covered in "Mondale '84" and "Dump Reagan" bumper stickers.

"You guys are college kids? I love college kids. I was a college kid, several times" he said punctuating his remarks with a throaty laugh.

"Look at the beautiful hardwood floors," Mrs. Cribbs said to keep us from noticing the large pile of crud encrusted dishes in the sink. Fitzhugh intercepted Mary Ann's look intended for me.

"I'll keep the dirty dishes in my bedroom if you guys move in" he said nudging me to laugh with him.

I forget the woman's name who lived in the next place. It was an unusual name with a C or a K that she said was Ukrainian. What I do remember was the cats, seven by my count, eight by Mary Ann's. Her home was an enormous litter box. We held our breath as long as we could then politely said good-bye.

Our final contestant, a Mrs. Mazzini, should be a case study for history majors like myself interested in turn of the century immigrants. Mrs. Mazzini came to this country from Sicily as a child and yet, even after seventy years in Pennsylvania her accent was still intact. She was clad in black and exuded sorrow from every pore.

The bedroom she showed us was currently being used as a shrine to her late husband. "He worked Philbin textiles" Mrs. Mazzini said proudly. That had closed 34 years ago so you do the math. His picture, taken in his forties, had been blown up and placed in what seemed like a makeshift altar with smaller replicas of saints and crucifixes all around and rosaries hung like macramé.

"When did he pass away?" I asked gently while Mary Ann disapproved.

"It will be 21 year, next November the 8 th ."

Would I want my wife to grieve for me for more than two decades after I passed on? Would I want her to be so devastated by losing me that she could no longer experience even moments of joy? Yeah, I guess so.

Anyway, there was no way we could take that apartment. Asking an elderly Italian woman to move her late husband's shrine was akin to moving a sacred Indian burial ground, sure to bring a curse on the interloper.

"We have to move in with that Bob Dylan poster guy," I said to Mary Ann over pizza. "We could keep looking."

"And stay with Todd in the mean time?"

She put her head down for once accepting defeat.

"Okay, but he has to promise to keep the kitchen clean."

We walked to Mrs. Cribbs' office to sign the papers then, we stopped at Karen's to pick up Mary Ann's suitcases. I had to get my stuff and the rest of Mary Ann's from my dorm room.

"I'm not going back in there," Mary Ann said.

"But I can't carry everything by myself."

"I'll get it with you" Karen volunteered.

When we entered, Todd was in his usual place on the couch. I nodded as we walked past. Karen and I packed in haste mixing dirty clothes with clean. I carried the trunk as she took the two smaller suitcases.

"Was it something I said?" Todd asked as we made our escape.

On the way to Fitzhugh's, Mary Ann's bad eye faced my scar, always a bad omen. "You're going to have to quit school and get a job."

"There are openings at the supermarket where I work" Karen said.

"He needs a real job. He needs to quit school and start working 40, 50 hours a week. We need to scrimp and save."

"What do you mean?"

"Scrimp and save. I'm using my babysitting money to pay the first month's rent, but we have our own baby coming and he has to provide for her," Mary Ann said talking to Karen instead of me.

"Are you getting a job too?"

"Me? No one wants to hire an expectant mother. You get a job and we'll scrimp and save."

Karen walked us as far as Fitzhugh's door and the three of us hugged good-bye. Fitzhugh helped bring our belongings up.

"I took care of the dishes," he assured us.

We dropped the suitcases and surveyed our tiny bedroom with one window and walls that could use some paint. I suddenly realized that we didn't have a bed.

Sixteen

Once again, Mary Ann slept on a living room couch, this one more stained and more aromatic than even the standard dorm room model. "My back hurts and I have a stomachache and the baby probably got a contact high just from sleeping on that thing" she complained. I slept on a garment bag that was unzipped and placed face down on that hardwood floor the realtor loved so much. My back pain had to be twice hers and my eyes hurt from lack of sleep.

After a lackluster shower, I felt only slightly better. Mary Ann picked out an outfit for me for my first day in the real world. We disagreed about the necessity of a tie.

"It makes you look more grown-up."

"I feel silly."

We went back and forth until one of us prevailed.

The news was on in the living room. I ate my cereal to stories of pestilence and famine and terrorism from the real world, a world that I was about to enter for the very first time. Fitzhugh emerged from the bathroom. He did a double-take when he saw me, "You look like a Republican in that tie."

The sun was up but ineffectual at this hour. I could make out the top of the college's administration building in the distance as I marched in the opposite direction. "I'm on my way to my first day of work at a microbrewery," I thought to myself. "I'm not even old enough to drink legally." I shivered uncertain if it was from the cold or the turn my life had taken.

I was curious as to what it would be like working in a microbrewery. Was there a certain recipe we had to follow to make the beer?

Did they keep the beer in giant vats? How did they get the beer into the bottles and how did they get the caps on? Would that be where I came in or was it all done with machines? Would they make me wear a hairnet and rubber gloves?

As I neared the building, a standard non-descript brick structure I had driven past many times I looked for an entrance. For some reason, I had pictured a front door. I would ring the doorbell, calmly wait for someone to answer it, explain my predicament and begin my shift. I didn't see a door, just a stainless steel sign reading, "Hesby's Premium Lager; Why Not the Best?" Why not indeed?

I followed cars turning into the parking lot. I got out and chased after two blue collar types moving towards the factory. They were arguing over whether or not hockey players should be allowed to fight.

"They're consenting adults. They can do whatever they want."

"That's the dumbest thing I ever heard."

"Excuse me, sir?"

The hockey fan turned my way.

"Who can I talk to about starting work here?"

Both men seemed amused.

"Do you see that gentlemen in the blue truck?" He pointed to a pick-up just pulling in. "I believe that gentleman can help you with this undertaking."

The guy opposed to fighting in hockey laughed and the two men walked away.

I approached the man in the distance. He had a moustache, a facial feature I've always found intimidating. I could see his breath hovering over the coffee cup he held close to his chest. "Excuse me, sir."

He stopped, sipped and said nothing.

"I was told you'd be the person to talk to about getting a job here."

"How old are you?"

"Twenty."

"You go to Philbin?"

"I did until last week."

"Go back to school, kid."

"My girlfriend is pregnant and I-"

"Congratulations" he brushed past me, "We don't have any jobs and I wouldn't hire you if we did. Now get the fuck out of here."

Thus ended my dream of working at a microbrewery.

I knew I couldn't come home empty handed. Mary Ann was right. We've got a baby coming and I've got to start bringing some money in. I'll scrimp while she saves. Diagonally across the two lane highway, I spotted an auto body shop I had never noticed before. They make good money, I thought. A red van beeped at me as I scooted across both lanes. I entered the garage.

There was noise coming from the back of a foreign car on a lift. As I waited for the noise to stop I thought about what I would say when he asked me about my experience with tools. I'd tell him I once helped my mother crowbar nails out of a plank so a blind man could fall through some stairs and break several bones. I suppressed a smile.

The noise stopped and once again I said, "Excuse me, sir." A muscular man emerged from behind the car. He also had a moustache but it was thinner and less intimidating than the previous one.

He looked around, "Where's your car?"

"I don't have a car. I'm here because I need a job. I'm a very hard worker."

"I'm sure you are kid, but now's not the time. I just laid off two of my guys."

"Oh." The tie was a nice touch though."

I went to a nearby bus stop, sat on a bench and considered my options. I suddenly felt like my mother, sitting, staring and thinking. This was new to me but something she did every day. She'd walk away mid-conversation to sit and brood and never once did my father or I ask her what she was thinking about. It wasn't until after my Dad died and my wife and I cleaned out their home that we found her diaries and discovered what drove her to her silent contemplative world. I often wish I had never found out.

The bus pulling up jerked me back to the present. It was moving away from town so I got up and walked in the opposite direction. It took me almost an hour to make it to the center of town. There had to be someplace in Millwood I could work. I tried the hardware store where Mary Ann and I bought the infamous wallpaper. I tried the camera store, the ice cream parlor and the pharmacy. Typically, they were usually polite when they thought I was a customer and less so when they realized I wanted a job. One guy was flat-out rude.

Their reactions baffled me. Weren't they in my shoes just a few months or years before? Didn't they once arrive at the exact same location asking the exact same question? How dare I aspire to become one of them?

I walked past the bakery. The thought of working side by side with Irene amused me but it was not a real option. I remembered the movie theater through the alleyway. It was a pretentious little theatre that showed one movie at a time, with an attitude that said "this is all we have, take it or leave it."

I had no idea finding a job would be so difficult. I'd been looking for one all morning. Don't millions of people have them? It wasn't like I was trying to break into show business. I'd take anything.

I grabbed a sandwich at the diner. They weren't hiring and even worse their soup was "three bean", none of which were tasty. It was the middle of the day. I couldn't just give up and go home now. Mary Ann would think I didn't care about the baby and couldn't handle the responsibility. Going home and admitting defeat was not an option, so I went to the movies.

The movie was a French film that was supposed to be funny. Funny in a "no one laughs but everyone nods" kind of way. I took my time getting home. When I finally did, Karen was waiting for me on the front steps chewing gum. When she saw me, she jumped up, waved her arms and yelled, "C'mon, quick, we gotta go!"

SEVENTEEN

Karen ran towards her car and yelled again.

"Rory, c'mon

I began running too but I didn't know why.

"What's going on?"

"I'll tell you on the way to the hospital" she said opening the driver's side door and spitting out her gum. We both jumped in the car.

"She lost the baby," she said, putting the car in reverse and backing up. I had a sudden urge to throw up.

On the way to the hospital, Karen told me everything. Mary Ann woke up with back pain and abdominal cramps. After lunch, she began bleeding, freaked out and immediately called Karen.

"I told her to go to the hospital right away" Karen said, "Your roommate gave her a ride."

"Todd?"

"No, not Todd, the old guy you live with now."

Right, Fitzhugh, of course, I don't live with Todd any more.

Karen screeched to a stop at a red light deciding at the last possible second not to run it. Karen looked over at me briefly, "Lucky for you I happened to come home for lunch between Bio and Chem. I even drove around looking for you. Where were you?"

The light changed and I stared straight ahead.

"I was looking for a job," I said leaving out the part where I spent two hours watching a mediocre French film.

She pulled into the hospital parking lot and we hurried inside. In the waiting room, Fitzhugh sat underneath reading a magazine oblivious to the crying infant to his left and the crying six-year-old to his right.

"Hey" I said.

He looked up, "Oh."

Still clutching the magazine, he moved to the nurse's station and cleared his throat. "Darlene, here's the baby's father."

Darlene was fifty with teased hair that was so blonde it looked nearly white. She stared at me for a full two seconds, apparently deciding if my penis could really be the one responsible for the current predicament.

"All right," she said, "Come with me."

She walked me down a hallway, entered a room and pulled back the curtain. Mary Ann sat upright on an examining table wearing a hospital Johnny. Her hair was wild and her eyes puffy, making her good eye and bad eye indistinguishable.

"Hi," I said, cleverly.

She looked at me without recognition.

"I'll get the doctor," Darlene said.

"Are you okay?"

Mary Ann shrugged, "It hurt so much."

She sniffed. "I started bleeding and then…" she began crying and shaking simultaneously. I didn't realize Karen was there until she nudged me to give Mary Ann a hug. We were hugging when Darlene returned with the doctor.

"I'm Doctor Miller" he announced. He said it as if we should have heard of him - almost implying we were lucky to have him. He was Darlene's age with thick glasses and rubbery jowls.

"Your…" he started to say "wife" and then caught himself, "The mother of your child has had a miscarriage. It's very common. In fact, it's impossible to know how many women have had miscarriages because many women have them in the first few weeks without ever learning they were pregnant. Of the miscarriages that we know about, 80% occur in the first trimester."

I nodded knowing that Mary Ann is comforted by statistics.

"What caused it?" I asked.

"A miscarriage can be caused by a myriad of different factors" he said, reciting a speech he'd given many times before. "It could be the result of drug and alcohol use."

I shook my head "no".

"It could have something to do with the structure of the uterus; there could be a chromosomal abnormality, even a snake bite."

"So let's see" Karen joined in, "last night, a cobra slipped in the window and bit her on the ass?"

"There is no reason to be sarcastic, young lady."

"There is no reason to be ridiculous, Doctor," Karen snapped back.

I sensed his speech wasn't going as well as it normally did. A gurgling sound came from Mary Ann's throat and the focus shifted back to her.

"It's always been my dream to be a mother. Ever since I was a little girl that was all I ever wanted to be."

Mary Ann burst into tears and after Karen nudged me again I put a limp arm around her.

Doctor Miller did his best to calm Mary Ann down, "Many, many women who have had miscarriages go on to have children, especially someone as young as yourself. The fact that your husband's sperm was able to impregnate you once indicates you're both capable of conceiving."

It felt strange being referred to as the "husband."

Mary Ann stopped crying or at least began crying silently.

"My sister-in-law," the Doctor went on, "Had three miscarriages and now she has two beautiful children."

Mary Ann looked up, alarmed. "Three miscarriages? You mean this could happen to me again."

The doctor quickly backtracked realizing he'd made a tactical error.

"A woman your age has twenty more child bearing years at least. I want you to come to my office this week for a full screening to allay your fears."

"Okay," Mary Ann said weakly, her fears not even slightly allayed.

"Call my office and set up an appointment."

He pulled back the curtain and was gone.

Mary Ann glared at me accusingly. "I'm never going to have children, am I?" Her face was contorted in panic.

That's not what the doctor said. He said you've got twenty more years to have a baby." "At least twenty," Karen added taking my side. Tears were once again streaming down Mary Ann's face. For a moment only noises not words came from her.

I looked helplessly to Karen. Mary Ann began rocking back and forth saying, "I'm never going to have a baby. I'm never going to have a baby."

"Yes, you will," Karen insisted. "I want one now," Mary Ann said.

"We can have one now," I said causing them both to look at me in surprise.

"We can?" Mary Ann asked.

"Sure. We'll start this week. I'll get you pregnant. It happened before, it'll happen again."

"Do you promise? Promise me."

"Yes, yes, I promise."

Mary Ann looked at Karen as her witness. "You heard him promise."

"We should get going," Karen said.

Mary Ann started to get off the table and then stopped suddenly looking at me face to face.

"Did you get a job?"

I hesitated.

"No" I said, "But I will. I'll look again tomorrow."

We helped her slide off the table.

"You know," said Karen, "It's a bit of a hike but I bet I could get you a job at the supermarket where I work."

I nodded agreeably.

"Okay, I'll swing by at 8."

We drove home with all three of us in the front seat and Mary Ann in the middle. Mary Ann was still somewhat catatonic so Karen and I each took an arm and slowly led her from the car up two flights and into the apartment. Fitzhugh was in his room with the door shut and music playing. "Almost there," I said, turning the light on in our bedroom. The three of us froze in the doorway.

"Fuck, we still don't have a bed."

Eighteen

The plan was for Mary Ann to look for a bed while I looked for a job. She was going to check the want ads and if that didn't work she'd buy a futon.

"I didn't feel well," she said pleading her case even though no one was accusing her. "I know I was supposed to buy the bed but my stomach hurt and I started bleeding from down there."

With all that had happened that day, the phrase "down there" struck me as so bizarrely prudish that I nearly laughed.

"I meant to get a bed, I meant to get a bed, I really meant to," and the tears and the shaking reemerged.

"It's okay, honey" said Karen as if she were talking to a small child. "It's okay, here." We brought Mary Ann over to the living room couch. Fitzhugh poked his head out from the bedroom.

"Everything is okay," Karen reassured him.

Mary Ann curled up on the couch in the fetal position.

"I hate this fuckin' couch," she barked. "It stinks."

The word "fuck" sounded strange coming from the same person who just referred to her vagina as "down there."

"It's okay, sweetie," Karen said placing a blanket over her. "Rory and I are going to go out and get a bed right now. We'll be back in a little bit."

I waited until we got down the stairs and outside before asking Karen, "Where the hell are we going to get a bed at this time of night?"

She kept walking with her back towards me when she suddenly turned, her face alive with inspiration.

"We'll take the bed from your dorm room," she said as we got into her car.

She was the first person I'd seen all day who was in a good mood. She turned the radio on and up and began to drive fast.

"How are we going to get the bed from my dorm all the way to my apartment?"

"Have a little faith, my boy," she said, patting me on the knee. I blushed suddenly remembering that she and I once had sex on top of a toilet.

Todd was on the couch when we entered. He laughed upon seeing me, maybe because I still had my tie on.

"My little boy's come back," he announced in a quavering voice imitating an elderly person, "He's come back, I tell you."

Dale came out of his room and seemed happy to see me. "Are you back for good?" "No, I'm just getting my bed."

As I walked into my room and began removing the blanket and sheets I could hear Karen talking to Todd and Dale in muffled tones. The word "miscarriage" wafted between the two rooms and hung in the air. I threw the sheets and blanket into a ball in the corner. Karen was now in the doorway, "The box spring won't fit in my car," she said, "But we can fold the mattress into the trunk."

We each got on one end of the mattress and got it off the box spring. In the process, I bumped the lamp on the desk with my elbow.

"You break it, you bought it," Todd yelled from the other room. We slid the mattress along the floor and without too much trouble got it to the front door.

"Hold it," Karen said opening the door a crack and peering down the hallway. She was short enough for me to peek over her head. A couple was having a fight just outside the room next door. The guy was losing. Karen shut the door so we could talk strategy.

"We have to get the mattress into the elevator without being seen," she whispered unnecessarily.

"What if someone is in the elevator or in the lobby?"

She didn't have an answer.

"I got it," said Todd and he got up from the couch and walked into the bedroom.

"Was he talking to us?" I wondered looking at Karen.

He was back almost immediately.

"Here," he said grabbing the mattress out of our hands and whisking it across the floor back into the bedroom.

"What are you doing?" Karen asked.

We followed him just in time to see him hoist the mattress up and propel it out the window. I rushed to have a look. The mattress bounced on the cement five stories below and then fell on its side with a dull thud.

"There," he said.

I scooped up the sheets, blanket and pillow and the three of us got into an empty elevator. "What if it had landed on someone?"

That possibility hadn't seemed to have occurred to him. He made a face and pushed "L."

"What if the campus police show up?" Karen wanted to know.

"They aren't real cops. Besides, those guys love me. I'm on the football team."

He spoke like an experienced mattress thief. The elevator door opened. It was late on a Sunday night and the lobby was deserted.

Todd carried his half of the mattress under his arm like a briefcase and Karen and I had trouble keeping up with him from the back. It only took a minute or two to reach Karen's car and bend the mattress into her trunk, no campus cops in sight. I felt exhilarated and wondered later if my mother experienced the same sensation when she unhinged the blind man's stairs and vandalized my girlfriend's home.

I let Todd sit in the passenger seat and I rode in the back.

"Why are you doing this?" I asked. "

I feel a little bad..." he said over his shoulder, "About puking on her."

Karen gave him a look but said nothing. He had always struck me as the least conscience driven person I knew, but I guess everyone has a secret side.

When we got there, Karen and I led the way this time with Todd pushing the heavy end up the stairs. Mary Ann was still awake on the couch and she bolted upright upon seeing Todd.

"What's he doing here?" she demanded pointing at Todd and ignoring the mattress. Karen, Todd and the mattress disappeared into the bedroom.

"We wouldn't have got it here without him."

Todd exited the bedroom and moved quickly towards the door.

"I still hate you," Mary Ann shrieked.

"I thought we shared something special," Todd yelled back and was gone.

NINETEEN

The next morning, my tie and I were ready when Karen pulled up at 8:30. I had been waiting for her on the stairs out front for a 32 full minutes. Am I going to be a responsible Dad or what?

"Did we agree on 8 or 8:30?"

She asked. "8:30", I said, to be polite.

I never knew how I was supposed to greet Karen. Was I supposed to give her a kiss on the cheek the way grown-ups of the opposite sex do? Were we supposed to shake hands like two business associates? What do other guys do when they meet a woman they've had sex on a toilet with and who's helping them get a job after their girlfriend's miscarriage? I jumped in the car and just said "hi."

"I called my boss this morning and told him I have a friend looking for a cashier's job. They need help during the day so unless you pee your pants during the interview, you got it." "Now you tell me," I said and she chuckled. It was always easier to make Karen laugh than Mary Ann.

She tried checking her watch without me noticing.

"What time do you have to be back?"

"I've got my Cognitive Behavior class at 10:30. I'll be all right."

Her driving contradicted this as she zipped through every light just before or just after it turned red. We crossed over from Millwood into Winton.

"This has to be about five miles from where you're living now. You might want to get a car."

"I can't afford a car. The whole reason I'm getting a job is to get some money so Mary Ann and I can have a baby."

She nodded, turned her head and looked away.

Burrell's Supermarket was off of route 134 with easy access for five neighboring towns. Its giant parking lot contained only a sprinkling of cars as we pulled in. Just as we were about to enter the store, Karen said, "By the way, my boss' name is Drake, he's a prick." I wished she had mentioned something sooner.

When we stepped through the automatic door, Drake was directing an old woman to something called, "Epsom Salts." He was balding, bespectacled and pudgy, yet his face was noticeably uncreased. He was one of those people whose age is difficult to pin down. He could be anywhere from his late twenties to his early forties.

"Drake, this is Rory."

His disappointment upon seeing me was obvious.

"You didn't tell me your friend was a guy."

"So?"

"You deceived me."

"I didn't deceive you. I said I have a friend who needs a full-time job. What difference does it make?"

"I don't like male cashiers."

Karen closed her eyes and squeezed the bridge of her nose between two fingers.

"All right, you win," she said softly, "I'll take him to the hospital and have his cock and balls removed."

Drake looked around nervously making sure no customers were in earshot.

"Very funny," he said finally.

"Look" Karen said breaking the impasse, "He can work as a cashier in the mornings and then when the high school girls show up he can switch over to bagging. You need daytime cashiers and he needs a job. What's the problem?"

He frowned but she knew she had him.

"All right, I'm having a girl trained at ten. He can be trained with her. Take him over to the booth and get the paperwork done."

Karen led me to something called the "Courtesy Booth" without Drake and me exchanging a single word. On our way, two cashiers, perhaps a tad older than us, gave me the once over and giggled. Out of earshot, Karen whispered, "They're lifers." She said this with gravity as though the two women were terminally ill.

Karen helped me fill out the necessary paperwork. The "girl" who was being trained turned out to be a 45-year-old housewife named Sally whose kids were now old enough to get themselves to and from school. They gave us name tags and orange smocks which signified "trainee." Karen showed us both how to punch in.

Christine, a 25-year-old go-getter, showed up to train us and Karen left me in her hands. It was like my first day of kindergarten all over again except that unlike my mother Karen didn't linger, refuse to leave, argue with the teacher and then eventually have to be escorted off the property by the principal and two of the janitors.

The registers were surprisingly new and featured something called "scanners." The idea was to bring the bar code across the electronic eye where it would beep and then the item would be added to the customer's total. It was actually kind of fun. Sally and I took turns; the trick was to find the bar code on each item. Sometimes you had to turn it in all directions to find it.

Christine stood looking over my shoulder. "Rory, if you do it like that it's going to take forty-five minutes to scan each item."

"I'm new," I said.

Sally and I spent the next two hours gliding practice items over the scanner and hoping for a beep. In between customers, the two lifers would look my way and make not so subtle comments.

"I think they like you," Sally said making me blush.

When it got slow, Drake would come by to remind us how important he is. He'd punctuate our mistakes with a "C'mon, Sally" or "C'mon, Rory" depending on who the offender was. The fun had worn off. After three hours, our training session was over and Sally scurried away hoping to beat her kids home.

I had to stay so Drake could teach me the intricacies of bagging groceries. It turns out; it's a complex process that involves putting heavier items on the bottom and more delicate ones on top.

"C'mon, Rory," Drake barked when I put too many items in one bag. "Dick Butkus couldn't lift that."

I seemed to get the hang of it after a while. He then took me outside and had me round up the shopping carriages.

"Pull'em back here to the front of the building and try not to get hit by a car. I don't want to have to clean up your corpse."

It was this kind of wit I had to look forward to forty hours a week.

"What the hell took you so long?" he wanted to know when I finished. "You can go now but be back at 9:45 tomorrow for your training session."

The lifers watched me walk out the door.

With some time to kill and uncertain about the bus route, I walked the five miles back to the apartment. As soon as I entered Mary Ann shut the TV off and stood up. Fitzhugh sat at the kitchen table chopping up onions. "Mincing" was the word he used. Man, that guy could mince. We exchanged hellos.

"Could I speak to you a moment?" Mary Ann asked leading me to the bedroom and closing the door.

"How'd it go?"

"Good, one more day of training and I'm a full-time cashier."

"That's good" then she whispered in my ear, "Let's do it."

"I was going to get some lunch. I haven't eaten since breakfast."

"You promised," she said and her large eye got larger. "All right, all right" I thought, "What's five more minutes."

We sat on my dorm room mattress and kissed without passion. She was naked almost immediately, anxious to get the new baby underway as soon as possible. At the moment of penetration, she screamed and I pulled out quickly.

"What are you doing?" she said, "Keep going."

"You're in pain."

"I'm fine."

"Why don't we wait a couple of days?"

"You promised me we could have a baby as soon as possible."

"I know but you're in pain. Why couldn't we wait a day or two?"

"You promised, you promised, you promised. Now let's go. I'll be fine."

I have to say I admired her courage. She was so determined to have a child she was willing to endure what must have been incredible pain. Most women will face the agony of child birth. Mary Ann was taking on the greater agony of conception. "She'll make a fantastic mother," I thought.

Reluctantly, I gave in. She grimaced and bit her lip.

"Just don't move and I'll be okay."

I tried to continue having sex while remaining as still as possible. She had on no make-up and the events of the day before still displayed their effects, her face tired, her coloring still pallid and there was peanut butter on her breath. Somehow, my penis lost interest and popped out. I could hardly blame it. I felt the same way.

"C'mon, Rory," she snapped reminding me of Drake and ruining the mood even further. "Concentrate."

I closed my eyes and thought of all the sexy images I could think of. Eventually, my penis came around.

TWENTY

We had sex four times that day. I'm not bragging, I'm complaining. If our bedroom had been equipped with motion detectors, our exploits would not have activated the sensors. Her vagina was raw and sore and I had to proceed with great deliberateness, each session more difficult and more time consuming than the one prior. It was sex completely devoid of sexiness. We were like Colonel Philbin and Old Nat, two statues one atop the other.

She finally fell asleep as I lay on my side of the twin bed. My penis, tired and tender, was grateful for the respite. I threw on a tee-shirt and sweats and found Fitzhugh sitting in the living room changing channels.

We nodded hellos.

"I want to thank you for bringing her to the hospital yesterday. That was a big help." "Oh," he said after thinking a moment as if six hours in the emergency room the day before had completely slipped his mind. "Luckily, I was home."

As far as I could tell, he was always home. He was perpetually unshaven but never bearded. He seemed somehow able to maintain a three-day growth at all times. His clothes were unkempt and unprofessional. His daily activities seemed restricted to the bedroom, the kitchen and the living room.

I sat down and worked up the courage to ask, "So what do you do?"

"Right now, I don't really do I just sort of be. I was an air traffic controller over at Latrobe and then Pruneface fired us all."

The air traffic controller strike and the subsequent firing by President Reagan was an event so significant even I had heard of it.

He was just getting started.

"I'll tell you one thing though. Never again will I suck on the corporate tit."

For the next fifteen minutes, he began haranguing me about the "corporate tit." About how his father had sucked on the corporate tit for thirty-eight years and it left him broken and bitter. His brother, he went on, now getting worked up, learning nothing from his father's life and continues to suck on the corporate tit despite having two heart attacks in his forties. "Everyone thinks the corporate tit will provide nourishment for themselves and their families but it won't."

It was more than a speech it was a soliloquy - one he had clearly delivered many times. I felt like a nurse at the old actor's home sitting at the bedside of an aged Shakespearean thespian as he played King Lear one more time. He spoke with passion and sincerity as if to a crowded house.

"The milk from the corporate tit has been poisoned. Instead of making us stronger, it weakens and enervates. The longer we suck on it, the fewer nutrients until it dries up, leaving us with emptied, bloated bellies."

He must have said the phrase "corporate tit" thirty five times in fifteen minutes. I wasn't a psychology major but this guy clearly has mother issues.

Somewhere in the middle of this rant it dawned on me, "This guy is really stoned." I later learned he rolled his joints with a mixture of tobacco and marijuana, a concoction he called a "t-bone." He smoked one every night, on the fire escape, at Mary Ann's behest. Afterwards, he became not mellow or giggly, but bitter and didactic.

"Why do you live here?"

"I grew up here. I went to Philbin for two years before they sent me to a little place called 'Vietnam.' Ever hear of it?"

This guy can't catch a break.

"Why did you come back here?"

"My mom started losing it," he said. (Ah ha! He does have mother issues!) "I had to put her in a nursing home, then the insurance ran out and I had to sell the house to keep her in there."

"I see," I thought, "The aforementioned corporate tit."

"Is she still there?"

"No, she died last fall."

"Sorry to hear that. My Mom died this January."

He got quiet for a moment. "We all go at some point, the hard part is getting to that point," he said laughing at his own wisdom. Maybe he is a little giggly after all.

It became clear that he and I lived lives under vastly different totalitarian regimes. His "Big Brother" was big government, a looming faceless asexual giant that didn't know his name and didn't care. My oppressor was feminine, intimate and psychological with a tiny queendom but just as formidable.

"What about you?"

"I just started working at a supermarket."

"Don't do it" he warned.

"I just need some money right now."

"Don't you see, it's the corporate tit?"

Mary Ann interrupted before he could get revved up again, "Rory, come to bed."

I obeyed, silently hoping I had run out of sperm.

TWENTY-ONE

That night I had a dream about Diane. It was the first time since my mother died. I used to have them all the time. For a few years, Diane had appeared almost nightly in my head like a Broadway actress on a successful run. The Diane dreams fell into two categories, the pretrial Diane dreams and the post-trial Diane dreams, the antebellum and the post-bellum to use Philbian terms. The pre-trial Diane dreams began my sophomore year of high school, a full year before I asked her out, and they were more romantic than sexual. There was always kissing involved but that was as far as it went. She was never naked and neither was I. It never occurred to my unconscious mind to conjure up her breasts since they were off limits to my conscious mind as well.

The pretrial dreams always followed the same formula. Diane and I were alone in a classroom, or on a picnic or at a lake or on a ski lift or (once, memorably) in a submarine. In each scenario, we would start out talking and end up kissing and that was it. The dreams weren't even imaginative by dream standards and until now, I never divulged their contents to anyone. I always awoke from a pretrial Diane dream feeling excited and delighted that the world offered good things and brought the hope of requited love.

The dreams continued even after my mother "allegedly" spray-painted "slut" on the side of her house. Diane had moved her seat in English class, stopped speaking to me or even looking my way, but the dreams continued right up until the judge's verdict.

My mother was the prime suspect almost immediately for one very simple reason, she was the "town kook." Her escapades, antics, tantrums whatever you want to call them were legendary. When you live in a small town you behave bizarrely at your own peril. I traveled in the backseat of her car with a knot in my stomach at all times, awaiting an impending incident.

A frequent object of my mother's wrath was a Mrs. Kim, a petite, arthritic woman who was the only Asian person in our town. My mother hated the Japanese for the injuries they inflicted upon my Dad at Okinawa. When she would spot Mrs. Kim walking down the street, my mother would roll down her window and scream "Pearl Harbor" over and over. Mrs. Kim would shake her head and continue on while Addison residents gaped in disbelief. When I got older I informed my mother that Mrs. Kim was actually Korean, a people who had more reason to hate the Japanese than we did. She shrugged her shoulders and kept at it. "It's a matter of principle," she said.

The incident with the blind man's stairs had emboldened my mother to commit another late night criminal act. However, the circumstances were vastly different. In the first instance, no one in our town knew that the blind man had hit me with a baseball bat, not even the blind man himself. There was nothing connecting me with Mr. McGinn. Here, everyone in my high school class knew within minutes that I had asked Diane out. Diane confiding in one friend was the same as announcing the news over the school's p.a. system. Teachers should consider spreading the theories of Pythagoras and Darwin as rumors if they sincerely want that information absorbed by their students.

However, it was not simply motive that brought this case to trial. Unlike her first crime, this one had a witness, Cal Dana, a man in his mid-twenties who called the police after reading about the vandalism in the Addison Sentinel. He saw a car of our make and model driving a few blocks from the Tracy home the night in question.

Under scrutiny, however, the witness' testimony became flawed. My father always said of the wee hours that only drunks and cops were on the road and Cal Dana was no cop. He admitted in open court to downing four drinks at the Town Tavern and another three at Tony's Pizzeria.

"You're lucky you're not the one on trial," the judge warned.

Our lawyer, Ted Gelso, was the son of a business associate of my Dad's. He was fresh out of law school and eager to step on whomever his career needed him to. Gelso pointed out that the term "slut" so integral to this particular case did not necessarily refer to Diane for Diane's name is not spray painted anywhere. The "slut" could be Diane's younger sister whose current boyfriend Jimmy Higgins was "no angel" in Gelso's words. Gelso even suggested the act could even have been the work of a jealous husband calling into question the fidelity of Mrs. Tracy. These tactics were angrily and summarily refuted by the prosecution but the seeds of ambiguity were planted.

When it was my turn, I simply testified that I didn't know anything. I didn't hear my mother get up and I didn't hear our car pull out of the driveway and I didn't hear it pull back in. I was sound asleep, most likely dreaming about Diane, although I left that part out. Afterwards, my mother never confessed nor intimated she was involved in any way. My appearance was brief and without drama, or so I thought.

Three days later as I sat in the cafeteria lapping up a fudgcicle, Diane confronted me. She was thin now, maybe even gaunt. Since the spray painting she must have lost fifteen pounds off an already slender frame. In a few short weeks, she'd gone from wide-eyed and cheerful to sullen and depressed. Shortly, after graduation her family packed up and moved never revealing where.

She stood before me barely resembling the girl I had asked out a few short months before.

"You know what your mother did. Why didn't you say something? You know what she did was wrong. You're just as bad as she is. You'll never be like Atticus Finch."

Two years earlier, I had defended Atticus Finch in a class discussion of "To Kill a Mockingbird." Tim Harwell said that Atticus shouldn't have allowed Bob Ewell to spit in his face; he should have stood up to him. I argued that by not stooping to Ewell's level, by maintaining his dignity, Atticus had stood up to him. For the next three weeks, Diane playfully called me Atticus before the nickname died of natural causes.

I had no response. What could I say? "I am so like Atticus Finch"? I just sat there foolishly holding my ice cream. She then walked away leaving that sixty-second encounter to haunt me ever since.

In the post-trial dreams, Diane invariably appeared as a skeleton spewing invectives to which I had no response. In this latest one, it was dinner for three with Fitzhugh, me and Diane at the table. Fitzhugh and I were eating delicious pies and I kept passing them onto Diane. "I don't want any pie, Fuckface, I just want a baby," she would say. She got thinner and thinner and turned into a skeleton. Suddenly, skeleton Diane was seated on a skeletal version of my mother and my mother was reading Babar to her on our red living room chair. Creepy.

The dream (really a nightmare) made no sense. Why would Diane be sitting on my mother's lap? My mother had ruined, if not her life, at least her adolescence and her outlook. I still wonder if Diane's weight loss progressed and became serious. I'll never know if she went to college or if she ever found a boyfriend or a husband or any man she could trust. Not all scars come from baseball bats.

My hatred for my mother became far stronger than any love I'd ever felt. My guilt over Diane fueled an overwhelming, all-consuming loathing. The sight of my mother, the sound of her voice, the very idea of her made my fists clench and my stomach involuntarily contract.

"What are you thinking about?" Mary Ann asked.

"Oh," I said, coming out of my stupor, "You know, what it's going to be like being a father."

TWENTY-TWO

"Where did you get that scar?" Drake asked after I had punched in. We had a free moment while Christine was getting set-up and Sally hadn't arrived yet. This was his version of small talk.

"When I was eleven," I said, "I got hit with a baseball bat…in gym class."

"That kid must have been quite a slugger."

I stood there silently with my scar facing him enjoying a long, tension-filled lull as Sally scurried in late and punched in. It seems one of her kids had forgotten his lunch and she had to drop it off before coming to work.

"I don't care about your spoiled little brats," Drake told her, "Be on time."

Sally looked as though she had been hit by a baseball bat.

It was day two of our training session. As cashiers, we were assigned a number which was logged in by Drake at the start of our shift. When we logged out at the end of our shift, the monitor printed out a sheet revealing how many items per minute we were ringing up and how much money we had taken in. The store accountant would check our balance to make sure it added up.

With solemnity, Christine finished up by discussing the importance of "freezing your register." Each of us would choose a five-digit secret code. "You are not to share this code with anyone not even your mother," Christine said looking directly at me, unaware that my mother was dead and equally unaware that if my mother were alive there isn't anything I would share with her.

"You will freeze your register when you go on break. If you have to assist a customer outside with their groceries or to help look for an item, you will freeze your register." Christine's eyes took turns locking onto Sally's eyes and then mine. "Freezing your register prevents you from being robbed. If you tell your friend your secret code, she could open your register, steal a hundred dollars and you would be held accountable. Promise me, you will tell no one your secret code."

Sally and I promised with all our hearts forever and ever.

Christine and I turned our backs while Sally entered her secret code then it was my turn. The code had to be five letters. M-A-R-Y-A-N-N was too long and R-O-R-Y was too short. I typed in K-A-R-E-N. No one would ever know anyway.

We were finally ready for actual honest-to-goodness supermarket customers. Sally and I were assigned adjacent registers while Christine stood in between and supervised. I was surprised how nervous I was. Not helping matters were the supreme interest that Laureen and Mia, the two lifers, took in my every move.

My first customer was a slightly built man in his mid-fifties buying cigarettes, hot dogs and a six-pack of grape soda. (Do grown men drink grape soda?) I missed one of the packages of hot dogs. Christine stepped in and saved the day.

"Rory, you have to scan every item."

"Sorry, I thought it beeped."

A few customers later, I charged a woman twice for a five pound bag of sugar. She barked at me while Christine did her best to placate her.

After an endless forty-five minutes, Drake came over.

"Scarface, take your break."

I started to head to the lunchroom.

"Whoa, whoa, whoa, freeze your register."

"Oh right," I said, surreptitiously typing in Karen's name.

Christine shot me a dirty look.

"I told him a million times," she said, pleading her case to Drake.

An hour or so later it was time for Sally and me to log out. She was going home to make sure her kids were still spoiled and I was to switch over and start bagging. Drake tore out my printout, "A good cashier rings up forty items per minute. Yours is eleven. That is God awful."

He then tore off Sally's printout. She had rung up eight items per minute.

"Mother of God," he moaned, "You two are the worst I've ever seen."

At three o'clock, Karen arrived for her shift with a chubby cheeked, bespectacled, young Asian woman who looked vaguely familiar. As I bagged some groceries, I introduced myself. She stared at me and said nothing. I suddenly remembered where I knew her from. She was one of the pushy virgins I let have sex with me during my promiscuous faze.

"You look different with your glasses on," I mumbled.

Too late, I had made the ultimate faux pas.

"What did you do to Lisa?" Karen asked me later.

During the pre-dinner rush, Drake was like a field commander directing his troops in battle. When he noticed a break in the line he would shift a bagger from one register to another. He marched back and forth imploring the cashiers to quicken their pace and face down the onslaught. Yet unlike Major Philbin, whose men by all accounts loved him and whose pleas for love of glory and country are well known, Drake motivated through abuse. He had a tailor-made, uncreative insult for each one of us.

To Laureen and Mia, he'd say, "Tweedledee and Tweedledum, move your asses." He told the Asian cashier, "Don't use double bags Chipmunk cheeks, it costs money." Only Karen, whose ring speed was a legendary sixty items per minute, was spared his butter knife wit. When he barked, "Hey, Scarface, go line up the shopping carriages," Karen shrugged sympathetically and whispered, "There's nothing worse than a tall guy with a Napoleon complex."

At six o'clock, my shift mercifully came to an end. On a windless evening, I found the walk home pleasant enough even relaxing after a stressful day. Just before I reached my apartment building, I heard one car door then another open and someone called my name, "Rory, could we talk to you a minute?"

TWENTY-THREE

I turned and saw Professor Jelinak standing there with pleading look on his face. Next to him was Todd with his typical expression that conveyed no brain activity whatsoever. I couldn't think of a more unlikely pair. It was like that weird photo of Nixon and Elvis. I froze and considered my options.

Jelinak opened the rear car door for me to get in. I knew I didn't have to go. He wasn't my professor anymore; I had dropped out of school. I could have told him to fuck off and there wouldn't have been anything he could have done about it. He couldn't force me to go anywhere that I didn't want to go.

Todd could. Todd was the biggest guy I knew. He could have grabbed me by my scrawny little neck and tossed me in the car and that would have been that. Yet, even this could have been avoided. I could have turned and run away. I could have run right up the steps into my apartment and locked the door behind me.

I got in the car. I rode in the backseat while Jelinak drove and Todd sat next to him.

"I know just the place," Jelinak said.

This constituted the only dialogue during the whole drive which ended at the diner.

Jelinak hummed to himself while the three of us looked at the menu. "The Greek salad looks good," he said as if everything were perfectly normal. As if the three of us old chums did this sort of thing all the time. As if this was some sort of a reunion instead of an abduction.

The waitress took our order with Jelinak asking for the aforementioned salad and Todd getting a turkey club. I ordered the spaghetti and meatballs. I suddenly wasn't hungry but I figured maybe I could spell out "Help Me" in the sauce.

When the waitress left, Jelinak leaned forward and whispered he wanted ten thousand dollars in unmarked bills. It took me a full two seconds and Todd a full five seconds to realize he was making a joke and by then it was too late to laugh. Besides, I wasn't in the mood anyway. He remained leaning towards me and got down to business. He said he was concerned because he hadn't seen me in class in several weeks. He said he stopped by my dorm room because he was worried about me.

"Todd told me you had dropped out," he said. "Todd and I are concerned that you're making a mistake."

With a straight face, he said Todd was concerned about me.

"I had to drop out" I said, "I got my girlfriend pregnant. She's Catholic and she won't have an abortion. I had to drop out of school and get a job so I could support her and the baby."

"She had a miscarriage," Todd yelled.

A few of the other customers looked our way. Jelinak looked over his shoulder wishing his beard covered his entire face. "Miscarriage" is one of those words that commands attention.

No one said anything for a moment. I noticed I had a plastic straw in my hand and was fiddling with it.

"I know she had a miscarriage." I said softly, "It was very traumatic for her. I love her and I promised her we'd have a baby together."

I was as surprised as they were to hear I was in love with Mary Ann.

"She's not even pretty," Todd said.

"You thought she was pretty when you were drunk."

"I think everyone's pretty when I'm drunk."

"Fellas, please," Jelinak said.

"You know what you are," Todd said, ignoring him. "You're like one of those guys who gets out of prison and can't handle life on the outside, so they commit a crime on purpose so they'll be caught and sent right back into the joint."

"What?"

"You don't want to spend the rest of your life with her, she's a bitch."

With the exception of the cook and me, everyone in the diner seemed to be enjoying our conversation.

"Okay, okay," Jelinak said, throwing up his hands, "That's enough. Todd, if I may?"

He sighed heavily and looked directly at me.

"Rory, you lost your mother recently. This is a profound tragedy for anyone especially someone as young as you are. You've lost your family unit and you're trying to create a new one. It's a very normal oedipal reaction."

I couldn't believe what I was hearing. I was the least Oedipal guy I knew. I didn't want to sleep with my mother. I didn't want anything to do with her at all. I had made a solemn promise to Mary Ann and I had to keep it. What else could I do?

"You and I can talk to the Dean" he said, "I'm sure we could work something out."

Now that I'm a teacher I've tried to model myself after Jelinak. I try and care about my students as people the way he does. Most of the time this means giving the bullshitters a kick in the ass. Occasionally, it means spotting a kid who's about to fall through the cracks and coaxing him along. This is why he was there that day.

The waitress arrived with our food. With some prompting she placed each order at its correct destination.

"Could I wash my hands?"

Begrudgingly, Todd let me out. I walked through the curtain towards the men's room door then slipped out the back entrance. I then headed home under the cover of darkness much like the army of Northern Virginia.

TWENTY-FOUR

It seems like my whole life it's been dinner for three. Before Gabriel was born I had no doubt he was going to be a boy. I somehow knew the pattern would continue, it's always two males and one female.

Growing up, dinner time was the time for settling scores. Wherever I had done wrong during the day was brought up and put on table along with our leftover chicken and baked potatoes. My mother spent the day gathering evidence against me and I was on trial every night at six o'clock.

"Is this true what your mother says?" my father would ask, "Were you running up the stairs when she asked for quiet?"

Gabriel laughs during dinner. Honest to God, he'll laugh right out loud in the middle of the meal. Where does he get the balls? I never did. He sits at the table like a sultan and luxuriates. He savors the foods he loves and we coax him through the foods he doesn't. Each night is a long, ritualistic extravaganza. I got my dinner over with as quickly as possible. There's a reason I'm skinny.

The meals I shared with Mary Ann and Fitzhugh were unlike any others. First of all, Fitzhugh was a terrific cook which surprised me initially but upon reflection made perfect sense. He may run an occasional errand or disappear for an infrequent appointment but the bulk of his life was spent in the apartment. His time was spent in his bedroom sleeping or typing away at who knows what, sitting in the living room watching the nascent 24-hour news channel or in the kitchen cooking. If you spent a third of your life doing something chances are you're going to be pretty good at it. Todd, for instance, is great at watching TV.

Fitzhugh's meals usually featured grilled chicken or fish topped with an elaborate homemade sauce and served with rice or freshly steamed vegetables. This was after a carefully prepared salad or some concoction with shrimp. For dessert, there would either be today's pie or last night's pie.

There was, of course, a catch. Since we were eating his food in his apartment we were subjected to his conversation. Night after night, we'd hear his analysis on the situation in Beirut or the fighting in Honduras. We'd be subjected to lectures on chlorofluorocarbons and nuclear proliferation. Neither Mary Ann nor I had any idea what the fuck he was talking about.

One night there was almost no conversation. Fitzhugh was normally animated and engaged, but this night, spoke rarely and in hushed tones.

"What's wrong?" I asked.

"Unspeakable tragedy today in Zaire."

"That's in Africa, right?" Mary Ann said proudly.

Unencumbered by a job or a woman, he watched and read and listened to the news all day each day. He seemed to know what was going on in every corner of the world. He spoke passionately against or in favor of leaders of countries I'd never even heard of. Since the news is mostly bad, it was not unusual to come home and find him weeping openly in front of a television displaying footage of earthquakes, wars or famine.

I was a history major. A year and a half of college had taught me about the Missouri Compromise and the Dred Scott decision. I had at least a passing familiarity with the abolitionist movement and what happened at Fort Sumter. I had trouble keeping up during conversations about anything that had occurred in the past one hundred and twenty years.

Fitzhugh hated his former employer President Reagan. It was always "Pruneface" this and "Pruneface" that. "Do you realize that he's going to be reelected simply because he took a bullet?" Fitzhugh would lament, his mouth full of Cobb salad, "That's the sum of his accomplishments."

Fitzhugh hated Reagan the way Philbin hated Lincoln. When the young Colonel returned from the war he was shocked to discover that his newly freed slaves had fled. He was stung by their lack of "gratitude." He had, after all, fed and clothed and sheltered them their whole lives and if he had subjected them to the lash it was "due to their waywardness," not his.

Ultimately, it was Lincoln whom Philbin blamed. His journals are filled with countless angry ramblings about the man he calls "The Slave stealer", an insult which has lost much of its luster in recent times. Even though Philbin grew far richer owning a factory as a northern based industrialist than he ever would have as a southern plantation owner, his venom toward the martyred president never waned. He found the bullet to Lincoln's brain "too good for him" and would have preferred a slower more elaborate punishment. Philbin was savvy enough a businessman and shrewd enough as a pillar of his adopted Pennsylvanian community to keep these opinions to himself and his private journals.

Fitzhugh was less circumspect, ranting about Reagan to any and all who would listen. Mary Ann and I were shocked. I had thought of President Reagan as a kindly grandfather, a genial old man who liked to ride horses and eat jellybeans. He'd never kill himself in front of his children the way my grandfather did. Sometimes we were tempted to argue with him but he had an unfair advantage. He was informed and we weren't.

My days were spent sliding groceries over a scanner and at night, I tried my best to impregnate my girlfriend. Fitzhugh provided my only mental stimulation. I looked forward to our dinners and even more to our late night talks when I would slip out of bed and find him high and more mellow but still proselytizing.

I was proud of myself in a strange way. I wasn't a chimp content to spend my days chasing orgasms. I was more than just a skinny body with an erect penis. I had a mind and I desired to learn about the world even if my teacher was an anti-social recluse.

One night, over dinner, he gave a long discourse on the Middle-East. He must have talked for over an hour. He explained the Israeli point of view, the Palestinian point of view along with a few groups I'd never even heard of. He went on and on describing what was going on and what he thought should be done. I understood maybe 60% of it but I like to think I learned a few things. After dinner, Mary Ann and I retired to the bedroom for some procreative sex.

"What did you think?" I asked her.

"Oh" she said, "I thought that pie was delicious."

TWENTY-FIVE

When I told my Dad that Mary Ann was pregnant, it took him a minute to process this information. It was as if the word "pregnant" was obscure and arcane like the words "matross" and "autarch" found in Philbin's diaries and he had to rack his brain to recall its meaning. When it came to him, a hint of a smile emerged on his face. "That's nice," he said softly.

Now it was my turn to not know how to react. This wasn't "nice." It was "un-nice." It was "anti-nice." It was in a separate universe as far from "nice" as possible. I had gotten a girl pregnant, a girl I would have trouble picking out of a police line-up.

"Why don't you help me get some firewood?"

He said, getting up from the table. We put our coats on and the cold air slapped us each in the face. He grabbed an axe from the shed and handed it to me handle-side first. I began chopping.

When I was little, once a week, nine months a year, I used to come outside with him and sit on a nearby stump and watch him hack away. He seemed so powerful to me then. The violence of the swing, the concussion of steel on wood, I was in awe.

Once, when I was five or six, I came home from shoes shopping with my mother to find he had chopped the wood without me. There were tears and a tantrum and recriminations. Even my mother took my side, the only time I can remember that happening. Not until I left for college, did he ever do it without me again.

There is no clearer bellwether for the passing of time than chopping wood. We used to hold the axe together so I could see what it was like. Eventually, he'd let me take a whack or two on my own and

109

then, gradually, a few more. By the time I was fourteen we were taking turns. At sixteen, the job was mine alone. It pained me knowing
that now that I was away, this older version of my Dad had to pick up
the axe once more.

While I chopped, he sat on the stump and pretended not to be
cold.

"I'll never forget when your mother told me she was pregnant with
you. I was so proud. She was so unhappy but I was so proud."

I stopped chopping.

"Why was she unhappy?"

"She was frightened, that's all."

I continued chopping and he continued his story.

"I came home from work that night and there was your mother,"
he paused and pointed at the ground with his arm, "lying on the living room rug crying her eyes out."

Some stories are better left untold I thought.

"I said, 'Helen, what's wrong? Are you hurt?' She said, 'I'm going
to have a baby.' I went to help her up but she pushed me away and
said, 'Don't touch me' and went right on crying."

My Dad laughed and seemed surprised when I didn't.

"I had just left Hackett and Wilson that December to start my
own accounting firm with Bob Jacobson. It was a very uncertain time
for us and I assumed she was worried about our finances but that
wasn't it at all."

"It wasn't?"

"No, no, it wasn't…" his voice trailed off and he became pensive.

"What was it?"

"Eventually, she stopped crying and I got her up and into a chair.
I got her some of that Earl Grey tea she likes. Liked."

He was not yet used to using the past tense when referring to my
mother.

She said, "What if he…I don't know how she knew you were going to be a he" he said, "But she did."

"Fifty-fifty chance" I thought.

"'What if he doesn't like me' Then, she burst into tears again. I had to calm her down all over again."

My Dad laughed some more and I leaned against the axe to catch my breath.

"I said, 'Helen, you're distressing yourself unnecessarily. Of course, he'll love you." She said, 'I stopped loving my mother years ago and I always hated my father's guts.' Can you imagine that? She was afraid you wouldn't love her and look how happy the three of us were."

I went back to chopping.

"She cried for quite a while that night. I think she finally calmed down when she saw how happy I was. A man my age, I'd almost given up on being a father. I figured I was shit out of luck," he said swearing for as far I knew the first time in his life.

"That's enough for today."

I put the axe back in the shed. I bent down and scooped up as much firewood as I could into my arms and started towards the house.

"It's a shame your mother isn't around to hear the news. She'd be so proud."

TWENTY-SIX

Over the next week and a half, Mary Ann and I fucked at least twice a day, once in the morning before I went to work and once in the evening when I came home. Occasionally, we'd squeeze another one in. I have to be honest…it wasn't bad. She was determined to get pregnant and who was I to stand in her way?

On Friday morning, while I was putting on my only tie, she told me, "Tell them you can't come to work tomorrow. We have to go to my parents' house for Easter."

"Is today Good Friday?"

"Yes."

I had forgotten all about Easter. Now that she mentioned it, I had a vague recollection of Drake telling us that everyone had to work on Saturday. Since I worked every Saturday I didn't think much of it. Now I realized, it was the Saturday before Easter and everyone in the five towns would be buying their Easter dinner.

Easter was actually a bigger holiday than Christmas in my house. My mother used to say that "anyone can be born but only Jesus can come back to life." Not that we went to church or anything but it was the one day a year we said grace and my mother would silently murmur some prayers and we'd have a pretty decent meal for once. Now that my Mom was gone, I hated to leave the old guy alone on the big day.

Her argument was that her family was more religious than mine therefore Easter was more important to them. Years later, Mary Ann was distraught when Gabriel rejected the Easter Bunny, "No, Easter Bunny…no." She tried to convince him otherwise, "Gabriel, the Easter Bunny loves you very much." "No!" He didn't want to hear it.

Kids are funny. He always loved Santa. He even half believed at eleven or twelve. While other kids cry and refuse to sit on his lap, Gabriel would tuck in and rattle off one toy after another from a seemingly endless list until eventually, Mary Ann or I would say, "Okay, that's enough," and pry him off.

It wasn't that Gabriel was afraid of the Easter Bunny, he was simply allergic to him, or assumed he was. He knew he was allergic to all furry animals. When he was three, Mary Ann bought him a kitten which he instantly loved even though in made his eyes run and nearly swell shut.

"He'll build up a tolerance."

"No, the only thing that's building is mucus. Say good bye to Sprinkles, Gabriel."

In kindergarten, Gabriel's class had a pet bunny for a few weeks. A few gentle pats the first day were enough to make his eyes hurt and the bunny's teeth frightened him. When the Easter season rolled around, Gabriel had a powerful sense memory. Bunnies were not his friends. If a small one caused this much pain, a six-footer was too deadly to contemplate.

"But, Sweetie, no one is allergic to the Easter Bunny."

Try as she might, Mary Ann could not convince him. Gabriel liked marshmallow peeps. He loved chocolate eggs. He was more than happy to hunt for them but he said, and he was quite clear, these treats did not come from the Bunny: "Jesus brought these."

Mary Ann had more luck arguing with me. "You have to come. I told my parents they'd get to meet the man I'm going to marry. My brothers will all be there. They can't wait to meet you."

After a minor skirmish I gave in. "I'll have to call my Dad," I thought.

There was still one major obstacle, Drake. Since everyone would be working that meant there would be no one to switch with. This presented a problem. I asked Karen for advice. "Just call in sick."

Right, as simple as that.

At the Battle of Gettysburg, the legendary Confederate General Robert E. Lee had explosive diarrhea. (Is there any other kind?) Whether it was caused by a touch of dysentery or the stress of the war's most important battle, historians don't all agree. All I knew was, if it was good enough for the South's greatest general, it was good enough for me.

The store opened at eight. At 7:35, on Holy Saturday morning, I called Drake. "God dammit, Scarface, it's the biggest day of the year."

I apologized profusely before and after he hung up.

"What an asshole," I said to Mary Ann, "I mean, what if I really had explosive diarrhea?" She continued packing her overnight bed.

"Did you know the "E" in Robert E. Lee stood for "explosive diarrhea?""

She stared at me blankly.

For about twenty minutes after I called in sick, my stomach actually hurt. I felt guilty about lying even to Drake. I convinced myself that if I had legitimate stomach pain than I wasn't a liar. I was someone who was ill and didn't want to spread his contagion to others. It almost worked.

By the time we arrived at the train station my mind had moved on. Two round trip train tickets to Dayton were more expensive than I thought and with the tax thrown in I was left with only a dollar and some change. Still, I felt like a man. Certainly, two weeks of fucking at all hours made me feel like a man but this was different. I had a job. I had earned money that I was using to provide for the woman who was to be the mother of my child. There was no denying it. I was officially a breadwinner.

Four and a half hours on the train with Mary Ann gave her almost enough time to say what was on her mind. I got the entire history of the Lange family. They were of German and Dutch extraction (Her words). Her Dad was a successful construction magnate (again, I'm quoting). Her Mom was a wonderful cook and very active in their church. She spoke of her brothers as though they were characters in a Harlequin Romance. One was a cop, one an electrician and one was a law student. Each one was handsome and muscular yet sensitive and a "real catch" (my words, not hers…just kidding, hers again).

As we jiggled across the Ohio border, I heard about every Lange family adventure. She told of their trip to Washington, D.C. when she was six and how she got separated from the others at the Smithsonian. For fifteen long minutes, her parents, panic-stricken, half-crazed with fear, searched "high and low" (mostly low I'm guessing) before finding her calmly sitting in the cafeteria eating an ice cream sandwich with money her grandmother had given her on the sly. The very same grandmother who played the organ at church and gave her a Kennedy half dollar for every tooth she lost.

I listened to stories of summers on Lake George and heard her tell of autumn afternoons spent apple picking and carving pumpkins and cold winter days filled with ski trips and tobogganing and hot cocoa. I was starting to see why Mary Ann wanted a family so badly. For her, family meant comfort and security and appreciation. I didn't have the heart to tell her that she was sadly mistaken, that she couldn't have been more wrong. Family actually means distrust and manipulation and control.

"How naïve are you?" I wanted to scream. Mothers don't bake cookies in the shape of snowmen and put Band-Aids on skinned knees. Mothers maim elderly blind widowers and shame teenage anorexics. Fathers don't spend hours playing kickball in the backyard and painting tiny furniture for their little girl's dollhouse. Fathers nod in agreement when their sons are demeaned and foster an environment of detached indifference.

By the time we pulled into the station in Dayton she had me convinced that she was right and I was wrong. She was so persuasive I felt lucky to be deemed worthy enough to enter her world. I had suddenly fallen madly in love with the exact same woman I had spent the last two months having sex with. For real. I mean how often does that happen?

TWENTY-SEVEN

Both of her parents were crying when they met us at the train station. Her father, a lion in autumn, called out, "Queenie!" prompting Mary Ann to squeal "Daddy!" She ran and jumped in his arms. He gave her a long bone-jarring hug as Mary Ann's mother and I stood by awkwardly shaking hands.

Whereas my Dad was slight and hunched and gray, hers was tall and expansive and blond. He looked like a clean shaven Viking king. He sized me up for a moment before enveloping my hand in his. You can't tell me this guy hasn't raped and pillaged.

With the introductions out of the way, he snatched up Mary Ann's suitcase and the two of them walked arm and arm to the parking lot. Mary Ann's mother, tall and slender, still with the remnants of a dancer's body trailed behind pleasantly chatting about the weather.

When we got to their station wagon, much to my surprise, Mary Ann rode in the front seat next to her Dad, with her mother and me in the back. The two in front had their own private conversation. They whispered and giggled and held hands at red lights. I was simultaneously jealous and creeped out. "Maybe I should get her back," I thought, "By putting the moves on her Mom."

It took us a half hour to reach Tilden. On the way, I counted five trucks emblazoned with the name "Lange." "I have a little something to show you" he said. I can't say for sure if he meant "you" singular or "you" plural but I have a pretty good idea. "Here it is, Queenie," he said, patting her knee as we pulled up.

We all got out of the car to stare at what was more or less a gigantic hole. Unoccupied Lange trucks of various purposes were scattered about.

"It's going to be a medical building" he said only to her. "We just broke ground."

"Oh, Daddy," Mary Ann gushed giving him yet another hug.

Mary Ann's home was more impressive than the hole. It was oversized and crisply white with clear bay windows and a circular gravel driveway. The front porch was supported by cylindrical pillars, (that's right, pillars!) and leading up to the pillars were twelve brick crowbar-proof stairs.

Mary Ann gave me a tour starting with of all things "the billiard room." "Where's Professor Plum with his lead pipe?" I whispered to her, nearly making her laugh. She was a tough crowd although her Dad seemed to have her rolling in the aisles.

Her bedroom, inconveniently placed next to her parents', had a lush yellow rug and bright yellow curtains and an eponymous queen-sized four poster bed covered in a menagerie of dozens of stuffed animals. It must take ten minutes to clear them off her bed at night and another ten to put them back in the morning.

"Here's where you'll be sleeping," Mary Ann said, "In Kenny's room."

Kenny, the electrician, still lived at home and worked for her Dad. He had, believe it or not, a trundle bed that pulled out from under his bed like an open-faced sandwich.

One by one, her brothers arrived home, first the cop, then my roommate the electrician, and then the law student. They weren't nearly as handsome or as muscular as advertised. The electrician was marred by the same wonky eye as Mary Ann. Each was big and burly. The word "oaf" comes to mind. They all probably played but didn't star on their high school football team.

That night, after shrimp cocktail and crab bisque, the grilling began.

"So Rory" her Dad said while carving the roast, "What are you studying in school?" "I'm a history major, sir."

"History? What the hell are you going to do with that?"

He seemed completely unaware that I had actually dropped out of school and taken a job at a supermarket in the hopes of impregnating his daughter.

Her Mom wanted to know if I was Catholic and seemed pleased when I said, "yes." The rest of her questions seemed less pointed. She asked where I grew up and if I had any siblings. When I mentioned my Mom had recently passed away her Dad softened a little and offered me a buttered roll.

After dinner, all of us watched a spy thriller in the den. Her father sat in a big chair in the middle of the room with Mary Ann on his lap and an afghan over the two of them. Somebody needed to break it to this guy that his daughter was no longer six years old. And by somebody, I mean somebody other than me.

At bedtime, I stole a kiss from Mary Ann on the sly.

"Your father hates me" I whispered.

"No, he doesn't," she said, pushing me away, "He likes you. I can tell."

I went to Kenny's room and while he brushed his teeth and what not I pulled open the trundle bed and got in. I lay there waiting for him like a nervous bride on her wedding night. Finally, he emerged freshly flossed.

"You're going to have to get up so I can get into my bed."

"Oh," I said.

I got up and closed my bed then he climbed in his and then I opened mine again. It was as awkward as it sounds.

He finally shut the light off and then he sighed and grunted a lot in his sleep. Each time he did, I would jerk awake. Nobody wants an overweight electrician rolling over on top of him.

The next morning, I joined them at the Easter vigil. Mary Ann wore a bright yellow dress and a matching purse. Her parents and the three oafs were decked out in their Easter best. I felt shabby in my all-purpose tie and had to follow Mary Ann's lead of when to stand and when to kneel.

In the parking lot afterwards, there was a lot of handshaking and kisses on cheeks. Everyone seemed to know Mary Ann and every-one wanted to know how she was enjoying Philbin. "I see" I thought, "This is what it's like to be part of a community." I'd never experi-enced this before. My family was the weirdo family. Our neighbors didn't wave and give us big smiles. When we left the house, our whole town suddenly got quiet and averted its gaze.

Back at the mansion, I shared in their endless supply of ham, yams, sweetbreads and pies. This was followed by a lazy afternoon of shooting hoops and shooting pool and gossiping about people I didn't know. At eight o'clock, when her Dad and brothers invited me to the local pub for a drink, part of me wanted to say "No, thanks," and turn in early. How different my life would have been if I had.

TWENTY-EIGHT

"Let's get the fuck out of here," one of the oafs said as soon as we got into the car. Now that there were no women present their personalities instantly transformed. These characters who for the last two days were soft-spoken and polite, almost to the point of being genteel were suddenly boisterous, profane and fun-loving. Loud music blared from the radio as the cop brother drove fast. Each of them began swear gratuitously. Even Mary Ann's father wore a mischievous grin.

We sped through Tilden taking shortcuts through side streets with almost no warning. We turned onto Main Street and came to a stop in front of a place called "Ned's Pub." It was one of a handful of store fronts in typical small town America. There was a bank next door and a Woolworth's across the street. Other than Ned's nothing else was open on Easter Sunday night nor I suspect any Sunday night.

Apparently, Ned doesn't work on Sunday nights because all the Lange men greeted the bartender as "Jackie." Jackie called each one by name even addressing the much older Mr. Lange as "Dick." No one bothered explaining who I was. There were plenty of seats to go around and our party huddled at a table in the corner.

"What are you drinking?" Mary Ann's Dad asked.

"I'll just have a beer, I guess. I'm not much of a drinker."

"That's what I like to hear" he said, slapping me hard on the shoulder, the first sign he was warming up to me. The electrician brought over a beer and a shot for each of us. No one seemed to mind I wasn't quite twenty-one.

The beer I could handle. The shot was unpleasant and burned my throat. The four of them laughed at my discomfort then the law student told the filthiest joke I'd ever heard. I laughed along with everyone else even though it seemed improbable that a parrot could be intimate with two women simultaneously.

One by one, the brothers and the Dad took turns bringing over a round of beers with a shot. The last one tasted like licorice. It was apparent this was some sort of initiation and I did my best to keep up. With each drink I was gaining acceptance into their tribe. I was becoming an honorary oaf.

They had done this before. Each of them moved about, played the jukebox, poked fun at the bartender, hit the men's room with great familiarity. "It must be a holiday tradition" I thought. From now on, I'd be spending Easter, Thanksgiving, 4th of July, Flag Day and Ramadan with the Lange men at Ned's Pub. I walked carefully to the bathroom and back. "We've got to teach you how to drink," the cop said to me drawing a laugh.

I envied the ease they had with their father. It was clear they respected and admired him yet they could elbow and tease him and he could give it right back. My father and I were never playful. We never shared even a moment of banter. How I wished just once I could get drunk with my Dad the way they were with theirs.

Having only a single dollar in my wallet, I skipped my turn on the round of drinks and the electrician went again. One of them said, "I want to hear how you met my sister." I don't recall which one said it because my mind was becoming fuzzy.

"There's not much to tell," I said, "We met through a mutual friend."

"Does this mutual friend have big tits?" the law student asked and everyone laughed. "Pretty big" I said, "I fucked her once in the bathroom on a toilet."

One of the oafs laughed with me.

"Actually, Karen was the one who brought Mary Ann to me."

"What do you mean?" her father asked. I told them the whole story, about how Karen brought inexperienced women to my dorm room and how Mary Ann became pregnant that first time. The jukebox finished playing and no one got up to plug in more quarters. I spoke without interruption. I told about the miscarriage and how upset she was.

"Don't worry," I assured them, "I love her very much and we're going to have another baby together."

Her father threw the first punch. I ducked nearly in time so his fist glanced off the back of my head. Though it vaguely hurt, I didn't utter a sound. I looked across at him, too stunned to speak. Then the cop punched me squarely under the eye right in my scar. I don't know what it is about that part of my face but no one ever misses it when they aim at it.

I was knocked to the floor, my chair skidding out from under me. Jackie was over the bar in an instant. His boots were near my head. I looked up at him. His face was flushed and his eyes intense. His arms were outstretched in front of the cop.

"I can't have this stuff in here. Take it outside."

I assumed the fight was over and that they had made their point but no. Much to my surprise, they did take "it" outside, the "it" in this case being me.

The back door opened and I was whisked out into the parking lot. One or two more punches were enough to knock me to the pavement. They then took turns kicking me, the law student being particularly vicious. I threw up after one hard kick to the stomach. Blood poured from my nose.

Finally, the kicking stopped. My head swam with the mixture of alcohol, pain and panic. "Throw this cocksucker in the dumpster," Mary Ann's Dad said.

"No" I screamed as I was lifted into the air. I tried to wriggle free. Moments later, I was thrown head first into the dumpster. I landed on a bed of overstuffed trash bags. I thrashed about for a minute or so and passed out.

TWENTY-NINE

The sun was already up when I opened my eyes. If you've ever woken up in a dumpster you probably have a good idea how I felt. The smell hit me even before the pain did. Why do all dumpsters smell exactly the same? They all can't possibly contain the exact same garbage.

The pain arrived in full force as soon as I moved. I let out a loud groan that echoed around the dumpster walls. My head throbbed from the deadly combination of alcohol and fists. I touched my nose, felt a sharp pain and cried out again. There was mostly dried, yet still sticky blood on my nose and chin and down the front of the shirt and tie. A lot of it.

I sat up but doubled over immediately from the pain in my ribs where I'd been kicked. I felt tears well up in my eyes as I clutched my side. Deep breaths hurt and in slow motion I tried forcing myself to sit up again. I knew I had to escape the stench before I did anything else.

I crawled over trash bags. I could hear bottles clinking together under me. The pain in my head, nose and ribs took turns pulsing through me. As gently and as deliberately as I could I climbed out of the dumpster, a sentence I hope to never utter again. The act of jumping down onto the pavement jarred my ribs causing me to yelp and lean over in agony. An older women passing by in her car witnessed the whole event. Her eyes got big and she scooted off frightened.

I walked away from the dumpster, bent over, breathing hard between gritted teeth two of which were missing. It was easier to stare at the ground but I needed to see where I was going. With great effort, I held my head up. I made it past Nat's Pub, got as far as the curb and sat down with a thud, much to the chagrin of my ribs. I held my head in my hands. No wonder my Dad didn't drink. I'm never doing this again, ever.

In my haze, it occurred to me that I needed to go to the hospital. I was pretty sure my nose and possibly some of my ribs were broken. Using a parking meter for balance, I stood up again. I walked toward a man buying a newspaper out of a machine. "Excuse me, sir," He turned my way, nearly dropping the morning edition, "For Christ sakes, kid"

"I need to go to the hospital."

"No shit. Go down here about four blocks and take a right on Elm."

I staggered past Quasimodo-like in the direction he pointed.

A young mom coming my way quickly hustled her two small children to the other side of the street. I plunged onward. After two blocks I saw one of those blue signs with the "H" for hospital and knew I was getting warmer. After turning onto Elm, the hospital was another half a mile away which is a lot when you're moving half a mile an hour.

At the emergency room, the middle-aged woman behind the counter's face puckered when she saw me. "Oh, my" she said quietly. Doesn't she see people like me all the time? This can't be her first day. "Do you have any insurance?" she asked after regaining her equipoise. I knew my Dad had a family insurance plan through his work. I could call him and get the information. But I couldn't. Though I meant to I never called to tell him I wasn't coming for Easter. The thought of listening to his silent disapproval was too much for me. "No" I said, "I don't." That seemed to be the answer she was expecting and she disappeared for a minute.

She brought back a nurse who was thirty-five-ish and almost pretty who told me come with her and I did. She sat me down on a table in an examining room and studied my face up close like an art appraiser. She shined a light in my eyes.

"You don't have a concussion but I bet that nose is broken. I'm going to clean you up and send you on your way."

Another blow I didn't see coming.

As she ran water over a wash cloth I figured out what I wanted to say.

"Can a doctor take a look at me?"

She shut off the faucet and wrung out the cloth while shaking her head.

"Honey, you don't want a doctor." She wiped my face while she spoke. "The doctor will tell you just what I told you. With his fee and an x-ray, it'll run you fifteen-hundred that you don't have."

I grimaced as she dabbed my face.

"It'll heal itself in a few days."

"Can I at least have an aspirin?"

She smiled a smile that made her look less pretty. "Sure."

Outside again, I made it to a bench and sat to formulate a plan. I knew I had missed my train but I thought if I could go to Mary Ann's house and get my stuff and my ticket I could go to the train station and they'd let me take a later train. All I had to do was make it to the nicest house in the nicest part of town.

I spent the rest of the morning walking to Mary Ann's house. Thanks to the aspirin my pain level went from "excruciating" to "slightly less excruciating." From time to time I would pause and lean against a tree to catch my breath. I knew I was getting closer. The houses were getting bigger. I turned down the street where I thought it was. It wasn't. It was the next one. Her house, a white monstrosity, stood out. I had found it.

I rang the doorbell.

"Who is it?" Mrs. Lange said behind an unopened door.

"Mrs. Lange, it's me, Rory Collins."

I waited for an answer. "Go away before I call the police."

Not the answer I was looking for. "Mrs. Lange, I need my stuff so I can get home, please. I'll just take it and leave."

She mulled this over.

"Wait there."

After a minute or two, the second story window opened, my bag was tossed onto the gravel driveway then the window was promptly shut. What happened to that nice Catholic lady who served me ham and hot buttered rolls only the day before?

Walking away, I searched my bag. It contained my clothes and my toothbrush but no train ticket. Our train home was scheduled for 7:28 that morning and I had given Mary Ann the tickets. She must have taken both of them with her.

Eventually, I made it back to the center of town. I found a pay phone and called Karen collect. She answered the phone. This was my lucky day. I told her everything.

"Shit," she said, "I'm supposed to work today. All right, I'll call in sick. Where will I meet you?"

"How about in the front of City Hall?," I said for simplicity sake.

"All right" I'll be there in about five hours."

As I hung up the phone, the rain began.

THIRTY

Normally I would have seen the dark clouds moving in but I was all hunched over and looking up was difficult. The rain started the way it usually does with great, big drops. Within minutes, it was a downpour. I took it personally. I was also hungry. I had expended a lot of energy walking to the hospital, across town to Mary Ann's house and all the way back and I hadn't had anything in my stomach (unless you count her brother's shoe) in several hours. I needed to get out of the rain and get something to eat. I picked up the pace and began sprinting two miles an hour.

I stopped momentarily under a tree and checked my funds. I had a dollar twenty seven that would have to last until Karen arrived in five hours. I decided to buy a couple of candy bars, maybe one with peanuts in it. That would hold me over.

Unfortunately, when you're soaking wet and you reek of puke and garbage simple tasks become not so simple. No one would let me in their store. As I entered a Mom and Pop shop, an old man who must have been the "Pop" scurried out from behind the counter.

"No, No," he said, wagging his finger at me.

"But I just want to buy a candy bar. I've got the money right here in my hand."

He wouldn't hear of it and pointed and pointed and berated me in what I think was Polish until I left.

Moments later, I was escorted out of a supermarket by Tilden's version of Drake.

"We don't allow no fuckin' bums in here."

I was speechless. One night in a dumpster and suddenly everyone thinks you're a bum.

I had similar results at the pharmacy and Woolworth's when I smartened up and found a mini-mart at a gas station. I was able to purchase two candy bars through the glass partition without having to go inside. The wind picked up and I began to shiver. I sought refuge at a nearby strip mall.

Although I had no intention of entering any of the stores and was content to wait out the storm underneath the overhang even this wasn't allowed. One by one, owners or employees came out and shooed me away from the front of their store.

"It's raining" I said.

Customers walking by were equally repulsed. Women my mother's age who probably had a kid the same age as me looked at me with pure hated. Then again, come to think of it, so did my actual Mom when she was still with us.

I became flushed with anger. I knew I smelled bad and looked worse but I had been beaten up. I was savagely pummeled by a cop, an electrician and a law student, not to mention a Dad. I was the victim and yet I found no one who viewed me as such. It occurred to me that there are people who suffer this indignation every day, those whose lives have for whatever reason taken a turn for the worse. "Why isn't society helping these down and out human beings?" I demanded to know in my own head. Never mind the "corporate tit," wait 'til Fitzhugh heard my diatribe on the plight of the homeless.

In the distance, I spotted what appeared to be another bum. (I now thought of myself as a bum) I was like a lonely moose discovering another moose in the Canadian Yukon after years of solitude. Without his knowledge, I began following him, the distance between us slowing narrowing.

The sun peeked out now but I was drenched through to my underwear and felt chills whenever the wind blew. My doppelganger, still oblivious to my presence, turned a corner. His black full length coat looked tired and torn even from a distance.

I followed him to the back of a warehouse where he stood upon a large grate with air flowing upward from it. "Do you mind if I stand here too?" I asked. He was hard to understand but I think I could make out the words "free country" amid some other ramblings. I stood next to him and the heat on the soles of my shoes felt good. I could learn a lot I decided from this wise old Indian.

Although an approximate age is difficult to pin down on one who's lived so hard, I guessed he must have been at least fifty with gray, sparse hair and a shaggy gray beard. His teeth were few and yellow and maintained a respectful distance from one another. I introduced myself but failed to catch his name when he mumbled it into his beard.

For the first time all day, I felt the joy of a kindred spirit. He and I were not bums I decided but "hobos." We had removed ourselves from society voluntarily to roam the land, make our own rules and have adventures in one town after another. This was the life we chose.

I tried desperately to establish a rapport but I couldn't understand what he was saying. I could make out a word here and there, "Cadillac" and "doughnut" for example, but whole paragraphs went right past me without comprehension. He was a loquacious, but inarticulate man.

Until the moment when he shit his pants, I was perfectly content on the grate. At first, I thought I must be mistaken, because he continued to stand upright and babble without the slightest change of expression, but very quickly, it became abundantly clear what was transpiring inside of his clothes. Although I stank of vomit and garbage, excrement tops both of those and I politely excused myself and moved on.

I spent the next hour and a half slowly circulating the perimeter of the City Hall as the sun turned in for the night. Finally, I spotted Karen's car and waved frantically until she saw me. When she pulled up, her shock and revulsion were unmistakable. "Jesus," she said, "Get in."

THIRTY-ONE

When I got in the car, Karen covered up her nose and scrunched up her face. I'm not sure what horrified her more, the way I looked or the way I smelled.

"I am taking you to the hospital, right now."

"I've been to the hospital. I don't have any insurance. They wouldn't help me."

She rolled down her window and I rolled down mine.

"All right then, I'm taking you to the police station. They should be arrested for doing this to you."

"One of them is a cop. They're not going to do anything. Can we just get something to eat and go home?"

She looked like she was going to cry.

"Please."

We found a cluster of fast food places and went through one of the drive-thrus. She bought me a couple of cheeseburgers and fries and a vanilla shake. My head still pounded and my nose and ribs throbbed but I felt slightly better. She gave me some ibuprofen from her purse and I washed it down with the shake, something I don't recommend.

It was chilly barreling down the highway with the windows wide open so Karen blasted the heat.

"Thanks for doing this."

She shrugged, "Anytime."

"What excuse did you give Drake for calling in sick?"

"I told him I had explosive diarrhea."

"That's the excuse I used."

"I know" she said, suppressing a smile, "He told everyone in the store you had explosive diarrhea."

Mortified, I shook my head and looked out the window.

"Don't worry, Laureen and Mia still love you."

"Well, they haven't seen me in a while."

"Or smelled you" Karen added.

I laughed until my ribs told me to knock it off.

I could feel my eyes getting puffy and with the heat blasting it wasn't long before I'd fallen asleep. I woke up a couple of hours later, disoriented and with a stiff neck to add to my list of woes. I could have used another hour or two in a nice comfortable dumpster.

The radio was playing softly and the windows were still down. I got my bearings. We didn't have too much more to go.

"Sorry," I said.

"It's okay" she murmured, "I just don't know exactly where I'm taking you."

"Could you drop me at my apartment?"

She blinked, "What if Mary Ann's there?"

"I'm hoping she's there. I want to talk to her." Karen seemed surprised but got off at the appropriate exit nonetheless.

She didn't say much as I thanked her profusely and exited the car. It took me two pushes to get the car door closed. "Sorry," I said again. I climbed the two flights of stairs all hunched over like Igor in a Frankenstein movie.

When I got to the top of the stairs I discovered my suitcase and my pillow in the hallway. My toothbrush and toiletries were tucked in the pillowcase. Of all that had happened to me that day this was the cruelest blow.

I don't know what I was expecting. I didn't know what her father and brothers had told her had happened. Maybe they told her I started the fight. (Can I even call it a fight?) I came there hoping she was worried about me. I was hoping she was on my side. I knew if I could just speak to her and she could see what they did to me I knew I could make everything okay.

I found the key and put it in the lock but the chain was on the door so it only opened a few inches.

"Mary Ann," I said, sticking my mouth in the opening, "Can you let me in, please? Let's talk about this."

"Go away," I heard her call from the bedroom.

"Please, c'mon, I can explain everything."

Fitzhugh appeared at the slightly open door. He flinched upon seeing my face.

"Rory, I'm afraid she doesn't want to see you right now. She needs some alone time to process her feelings."

"I just need to talk to her."

"I think you need to respect her rights as a woman and respect the boundaries she's established for your relationship."

"Please, can you ask her to just give me a few minutes to explain my side of the story?"

"I'll ask her."

He left me alone in the hallway for a minute or two. When he returned to the crack in the door he apologized, "Sorry, Rory," He began recounting everything that she said on his fingertips. "She never wants to see you again, she hates your guts, you were the biggest mistake of her life and if you don't leave she's going to call the police."

I had had enough encounters with the police for one day. Slowly, I picked up my stuff and walked back outside.

To my astonishment, Karen was still sitting in her car out in front of my building.

"She didn't want to see me," I said.

"I had a feeling," Karen said and I threw my things in the back seat. "Where do you want to go?"

I considered my options for a few moments.

"If you want you can come back and stay with me."

I looked at her out of the corner of a puffy eye.

"On the couch, I mean."

"I think I'll go back to my dorm and stay with Todd."

"Really?"

"It's still half my room."

"There's no bed."

"But there's a box spring. I can put a sleeping bag on top of the box spring."

We rode a few blocks in silence.

"I'm going to get her back," I said.

Karen said nothing.

"I love her," I said. "I love her so much and I'm going to do whatever it takes to get her back."

THIRTY-TWO

When I entered my dorm room Todd was laying on his bed masturbating. Each of us recoiled in horror.

"What the fuck!" he yelled, pulling up his boxer shorts as I ducked back behind the door. "Is it safe?" I asked.

"Hold on a second. I was just giving little Todd some air...okay, you can come in." Cautiously, I re-entered. He had put on gym shorts. He stared at me like I was an abstract painting.

"What the fuck happened to you?"

I shrugged and pulled a towel out from a drawer. I was becoming used to having this effect on people.

He stood up to get a closer look.

"Whoa," he covered his nose with his hand. "You smell like a French skunk's asshole." "He must have heard that somewhere," I thought. "I know," I said, "Sorry." I entered the bathroom, turned on the shower and closed the door.

I spent the next twenty minutes washing off blood and puke and garbage. I soaped and re-soaped my entire body and shampooed and re-shampooed my hair. I would have scrubbed my soul if I could. My nose and ribs stung even under the force of a lackluster current.

Toweling off, I summoned up the courage to wipe away the steam from the mirror and take a peek. What I saw would have made Laureen and Mia weep. Both of my eyes had swelled and were nearly shut. My nose bulged in the middle the way a snake's body does after consuming a wild boar. There was a deep bluish, purplish bruise along my scar and a reddish one along my jaw line. I stared for a full minute feeling sorry for the poor bastard looking back at me.

Finally, I reached down into my soiled clothes and plucked out my tie. It being the only one I had I washed off the blood as best I could and left it hanging over the shower curtain. I took two more aspirin and opened the door a crack. The room was empty. I got dressed.

With Todd back in his usual spot on the couch, I took a plastic trash bag from under the sink and filled it with my Easter clothes.

"Wait, where are you going?" Todd yelled, a hint of panic in his voice.

"Don't worry, I'll be right back."

I took the elevator downstairs. In the lobby, I saw a guy I kind of knew from my Psych class. His name was Justin or Jason. He always had his hand up asking probing questions. He averted his gaze as I walked past. Even the intellectually curious didn't want to know what had happened to me.

I walked outside to the back of the building. I opened up the dumpster lid and heaved the bag of clothes inside. I again smelled that smell that all dumpsters have. I put the lid back down. "I slept in one of those last night" I thought as I re-entered my dorm.

After losing his hand, Major Philbin was out of commission for a while. He returned home to his beloved North Carolina and drank and convalesced and sank into a bitter depression. After four long months, he snapped out of it and as a Colonel had a hand (a right hand!) in the battles of Wilderness and Petersburg.

This was to be my recovery period. Sleeping back in my dorm room would allow me to live rent free. My face would heal and I would continue to go work every day and I could put together a little nest egg. I knew Mary Ann desperately wanted a child. How could she say "no" to a guy with money in his pocket and a healed face? My plan to win her back was already underway. The South shall rise again.

When I got back, Todd was in the kitchen putting some ice cubes in a baggie for me.

"I must look pretty bad if you're helping me," I said.

"Why would you say that?," He asked, "I'm a thoughtful person."

Don't tell me I hurt his feelings. No one is safe on this day.

I draped the ice pack around a dish towel and put it on my face.

"I want to hear the whole story," he said, "Wait, I want some ice cream first."

He took a carton from the freezer and scooped some ice cream into a large bowl. I sat on a couch in the living room and waited for him.

He sat across from me on his couch with the bowl in his lap.

"All right, let's hear it." I told him everything.

I didn't edit out any of the details as I did for Karen. I recalled every punch and each kick. Once or twice, he looked like he was about to say something but changed his mind. He let me ramble on and on.

When I finished, Todd shook his head and we sat silently for a little bit taking in all that had happened. He sucked in one spoonful after another.

"Do you want me to beat them up for you?"

"You can't, one of them's a cop," I said, appreciating the sentiment. Maybe he is a thoughtful person.

"So you're going back to class tomorrow?"

"I can't go back looking like this. I'd frighten all the girls."

He jabbed the air with his spoon, "You got a point there."

I told him my plan for winning Mary Ann back. A wry smile came over his face as he finished off the bowl.

"You never disappoint," he said.

THIRTY-THREE

I was late for work the next day. With all my mind and body had been through the day before a long, deep sleep on a box spring with three balled up sweatshirts as a pillow was just what I needed. I hurried along not really running because the pounding was too much on my ribs.

When I entered the store, Laureen looked past her customer at me and then looked quickly at Mia. The two of them were heart-broken. If I could have I would have hired someone to come in and warn them before I made my entrance. I thought Laureen was going to cry. I put my head down and walked over to where Sally stood talking to Drake.

"Listen, Sally," Drake said, in full lecture mode, "I understand he's got a fever but you've got a job to do."

Sally's face wore a worried look.

"I just think I should be with him. He's only seven and he's ill."

"Are you a registered nurse?"

Sally didn't answer and the two of them had still not looked my way.

"Okay, then, he's with a trained nurse. You can leave here when your shift is over at one o'clock."

Sally seemed on the verge of tears when she turned and saw my face, "Oh, Rory, what happened?"

Drake noticed me now. He was instantly angry.

"Scarface, what the hell? I can't put you on a register looking like that."

"I got into a car accident," I mumbled, having devised that excuse on the way over. The old, "My girlfriend's family beat me up and then stuffed me in a dumpster" excuse seemed too…well, you know.

"You must be in so much pain" Sally said in a motherly voice, not like my mother's but a normal mother's.

"Sally, please unfreeze your register and get back to work" Drake snapped. "Come with me," he said leading me down the dairy aisle. "You're going to have to work in dairy. I can't have you ringing up people's food looking like that."

He brought me through the swinging doors to the loading dock. "I'm going to have to call you 'Scars-face' from now on," he said with a chuckle.

I spent the rest of the week in the dairy department. I loaded and unloaded milk. Customers could still see me while I placed the milk on the shelves but I guess since I wasn't dealing with them directly it was okay. Half the time I was stuck wearing a winter coat and putting the ice cream in the freezer. I was like a creature chained in the basement by the mad scientist.

When my black eye faded to a yellowish hue, I was allowed back into society. I must have looked presentable because Laureen and Mia went back to whispering about me between customers. Drake continued to ride Sally about her dismal ring speed while mine rose to a respectable 35 items per minute and my life moved ahead at a glacial pace.

I worked overtime whenever I could because it paid me one and a half times the hourly wage. I would come home exhausted, endure a few wisecracks from Todd, fall asleep on the box spring and do it all again. My nest egg grew to a little over five hundred dollars, the most money I'd ever had at one time.

"Too bad you can't put that money under your mattress," Todd pointed out.

It's funny that when I thought about Mary Ann, which was all the time, I didn't dwell on the beating or the dumpster or any of the bad stuff. What I kept thinking about was the dinner on Easter Sunday and how her family enjoyed being together. Never mind the beautiful house and the delicious food, there was laughter and affection and good will. That was what I wanted. I wanted to be part of that again. I wanted what had happened at the bar to be something we'd laugh about years from now when Mary Ann and I were back together. With each pay check, I felt closer to her. Each envelope was proof of my suitability as a father. Each week, my optimism increased and I felt more and more confident that I could win her back.

After a long demoralizing snowy Pennsylvania winter and an equally demoralizing rainy Pennsylvania spring, summer suddenly showed up unannounced in mid-May. Barbecues and picnics were hastily arranged and the store overflowed with customers in desperate need of burgers and watermelon and potato salad. I had never seen the store so crowded.

Karen arrived at noon with all six cash registers fighting to hold off wave after wave of would-be barbecuers. After a week and a half of finals, she was bleary-eyed and haggard and for the first time I ever saw her skin was badly broken out. She wore a pair of Capri slacks that didn't flatter her. She kept her head down and didn't look my way.

"When did you become a Zitface?" Drake asked in lieu of "Hello."

Drake directed Karen to the express register next to mine where the line was the longest, opting to use his fastest gun to protect his flank. "Move your fat ass," he told her unconcerned that customers could hear him. Breaks were canceled and we all bore down to face the barrage.

Saturdays were usually crowded. The pattern on Saturdays was always rush then lull, rush and then lull. On this day there was no lull. It was as if the people exiting put their groceries into their cars and then reentered the store, picked up more groceries and got back in line. Philbin wrote about "the infinite and grievous enemy who did not want of supply." We now faced a similar foe.

Karen had the worst of it. The line at the express register now stretched into one of the aisles. Customers running in to pick up one or two indispensable items had to wait as long as forty-minutes and it made them angry. Karen, stressed out and sleep deprived from finals, was not up to the task. A woman yelped when Karen handed her the wrong change, twenty-seven cents instead of seventy-two.

"What are you, a retard?" Drake asked.

I avoided eye contact with her as I handed a customer his milk.

I wanted to offer encouragement but I had my own long line of angry customers to deal with. I overheard an old man on his way out grumble to Drake about the slow moving cashier at register one. Drake, with eyes narrowed, barked at Karen "pick up the pace, Zit-face." Tears slid down her reddened face.

"That is enough," I screamed suddenly.

Co-workers and customers froze.

"Rory," Sally said softly from the next register. I could feel my ears become warm and the voice coming from me didn't sound like my own. It was throaty and deep and filled with emotion.

"We are sick of this!"

Drake stood open mouthed unsure of what was happening.

"Freeze your register," I told Karen. I turned to Sally, "Freeze your register!" I commanded. I then froze mine.

"Rory, get back to work" warned Drake.

I raced towards Laureen and Mia. "Freeze your registers!" I yelled.

"What the hell is going on?" a customer asked.

"Rory, Rory" Drake pleaded, his path toward me blocked by customers. By now, Laureen and Mia had done as they were told and looked at me for further instructions.

"We're leaving," I said having successfully shut down five of the six registers.

"Get back to work" Drake screamed, but Karen, Sally, Laureen and Mia were now right behind me.

The last cashier was Lisa. Just my luck. Why couldn't it be some-one who'd lost her virginity to somebody else?

"Lisa!," I said, desperately, "Freeze your register."

"Don't do it!" Drake yelled.

Lisa looked from me to Drake and back again trying to decide who she hated more.

"Do it," Karen yelled.

"Sorry," Lisa shrugged to her customer as she turned and typed in her secret code.

All six of us now were at the exit. Drake grabbed me and spun me around, his eyes wild with fear and anger. He grabbed my lapel with his right hand and my tie with his left. We grappled Greco-Roman style out the automatic door, two wimps locked in mortal combat. A slap fight might break out any second now. He spun me around gain-ing the upper hand, then, as he began to pull me back towards the store, Karen kicked him hard and without mercy right in the crotch. He let out a screech and fell to the pavement.

"This way" Karen yelled and all six of us ran to her car. We quickly piled in three in front and three in the back. Karen backed out and sped off as though we had just robbed the place. We hooted and howled and laughed and cheered.

"We did it!" Sally yelled. We sure did.

THIRTY-FOUR

We dropped off Laureen first and then Mia. I gave them each a hug. I now had second thoughts. The two of them had a crush on me and I repaid them by making them give up their jobs, their full-time jobs.

"They're better off" Karen said, "They don't want to do that their whole lives."

She was right. I had freed them; I was a poor man's Abe Lincoln.

When we pulled up in front of Sally's house, Sally began to giggle. Instead of getting out the car, she stayed in the backseat, bent over, laughing uncontrollably. Karen and I exchanged quizzical looks 'til Sally finally let us in on the joke.

"I drove to work today" she said. Then we laughed though not as hard as Sally.

"Do you want me to bring you back to the store?" Karen asked.

"No, that's okay. My husband can bring me."

We said our good-byes and she got out of the car, a nice lady who didn't belong in a supermarket.

Karen drove off with me in the front seat and Lisa still in the back.

"Can you drop me in town?" Lisa asked, the first words she had spoken since she got in the car. "Are you sure?" Karen said.

"Yeah, I have some errands to run."

I wondered if she had second thoughts. None of us spoke for several minutes. "Thanks," Lisa said cheerfully when Karen pulled over in Millwood center.

"Bye" I said.

"Bye" Lisa replied.

That was big of her.

Karen and I drove off alone. Somewhere along the way, Karen and I had telepathically decided to go back to her dorm to fuck. She drove, silently and purposely to the campus and parked in front of her building. We exchanged sly smiles as we entered her building and began making out in the elevator.

When we got to her room, her roommate was packing to head home for the summer. She was the pretty one to whom I'd lost my virginity. Her hair was pulled back in a ponytail and she wore an oversized man's football jersey. She looked at me blandly without any hint of recognition. Karen asked me to "give them a minute" and I went to the kitchen for a glass of water.

After a few moments of murmuring I heard Karen yell, "I slept on the couch for you a hundred times you selfish bitch!"

Almost immediately, her roommate stormed past me and out the door. I entered Karen's room. She lifted her hands towards the ceiling, "How's that for romantic?"

Then for the first time ever, Karen and I had non-toilet seat related sex. Though she didn't look too good and I still didn't look too good all the adrenalin from the supermarket rebellion propelled us into passionate, lustful, satisfying sex.

Afterwards, we lay on our backs sweating and panting and wordlessly processing the day's bizarre events. A warm breeze wafted through an open window. After a long pause, Karen broke the ice, "So what the fuck happens now?"

"I don't know," I said, "I guess your Dad and brothers beat the shit out of me."

She began laughing and then I began laughing. When one of us stopped the other continued and soon we were both laughing again. We laughed to relieve the weirdness. It's probably what Sally was doing.

One of the innumerable benefits of youth is that the intervals between sex are brief and a few minutes later we were at it again with her on top this time. Our bodies were in sync and if a Peeping Tom were watching he'd swear the two of us knew what we were doing.

When we were finished, my body worn out and proud of itself succumbed to the warm breeze and I dozed off. I awoke when her roommate pounded on the door.

"Karen, she said formally, "May I please come in and pack. My parents are coming tomorrow morning."

"Just a minute" Karen yelled back.

We dressed quickly and she opened the door.

Karen took the high road. "Laura, this is Rory."

"Hello, Rory" Laura said evenly, "Nice to meet you."

Did she really not know me? Or was it an act? I couldn't tell. I stood silently pretending not to notice how pretty she was. "Let's get a bite," Karen said and I followed her into the kitchen.

With the school year all but over we were left with random items from a picked over refrigerator and nearly empty cabinets. We dined on graham crackers and English muffins and cheese whiz. It was glorious.

When it got dark, Karen brought me to an end of the semester party, a final blow-out before everyone went home for the summer. We drank beer from a keg in plastic cups and talked over loud music. We even held hands once I looked around and made sure Mary Ann wasn't there.

Being with Karen was like having a girlfriend and hanging out with a guy at the same time. In the first place, she could drink more than I could. At the party, she had five beers to my three and (unlike me) seemed completely unaffected. Secondly, she liked to greet people with, "How the fuck are you?" It's something she'd done ever since we'd met. It never bothered me before but now that we were becoming girlfriend and boyfriend I didn't know what to think. My mother never swore. I think I'd heard Mary Ann swear once, maybe twice but that was it. Karen wasn't the type of girlfriend I was expecting when I went looking for one.

As the night wore on I began to relax and I realized I was actually having fun. Towards the end of my third beer I even felt a surge of joy. It was the joy of feeling normal. Sure a few people asked, "Where have you been?" and things of that nature but for the most part I blended right in. I was doing what a typical college student does even though I hadn't been to class in eight weeks. For once, I was basking in the joy of a normal life.

As a child, I did my best to study "normal" kids and copy their behavior. I was always terrified that I wasn't dressed correctly. I was never sure if I was standing or sitting the right way. I was certain people could look at me and instantly tell that I was born in a freak show the spawn of two mutants.

When Gabriel was little, his teachers would describe his behavior as "age appropriate" a term people never use when describing adults. When a forty something year old man purchases a sports car during a mid-life crisis no one uses the term "age appropriate." Yet, everything Karen did, the way she dressed and swore and the things she liked and disliked all seemed to be the right thing at the right time. I followed her lead.

When she brought me back to her place that night I did as I was told. We lay side by side sexlessly respecting the fact that Laura was asleep nearby. I had never slept in the same room with two women I had had sex with before. It may sound erotic but it wasn't. Laura didn't even remember me but I knew Karen knew and it made me uneasy.

In the morning, Karen and I pretended to be asleep as Laura shoved her suitcases out the door. I could hear her Dad's voice and not until they were safely gone did either of us stir. "We have time before my parents come," Karen said with a mischievous grin.

When we finished, she whispered in my ear "I love you" and a wave of fear washed over me. What possessed her to say such a thing?

I grew up in a house where people didn't say that word to each other. If someone said the word "love" it was followed by the word "candy" or "ice cream" or "cake." It was a word I only associated with inanimate objects not something said from one person to another. She looked over at me, awaiting a response. I nodded.

"That's all I get? A fuckin' nod?" For the second time in two days, my voice sounded like someone else's. This time it was quavering and strangely high-pitched, "I...um...I... you know..."

She sat up. "You should go," she said, "My parents will be here soon."

THIRTY-FIVE

I retreated to my dorm room. It was the final weekend of the school year and people moved pell-mell across a crowded campus. Students, who just a few hours earlier were drunk and coital, accompanied by their parents and now acted sober and chaste. Young and old carried suitcases and boxes. Somebody's Mom walked past me with a bird cage. I saw people hugging and more than once, I heard someone yell, "See you in September!" through an open window.

When I got back to my room, Todd was awake but still lying in bed. He was shirtless and he sat up upon my entrance. His man boobs jiggled.

"Look who was out all night. Don't tell me you're once again impregnating the class of '84?"

I chuckled and moved towards the shower. He wasn't done.

"So are you back with your girlfriend?"

I shook my head "no."

"Oh, how in-ter-est-ing," he said adding a hyphen to each syllable for dramatic effect. "I don't know if I approve of you seeing someone I haven't thrown up on."

I showered and had an orange. Since Todd was packing I decided to do the same. For some reason, he didn't have any suitcases and was putting all of his clothes into large green trash bags. He had sold his textbooks back to the bookstore and he threw away his notebooks.

"Aren't you going to need those?" I asked.

"What for?" he said, "There's nothing in there but doodles."

Early that afternoon, his parents arrived. I hadn't met them when the school year started as I had shown up late in the day. Like him, they were wide and slovenly. His mother looked more like a female impersonator than an actual woman. Her hair was a dark exaggerated beehive and her hands were huge and mannish. His father was overweight and slow moving. His jowls sagged and he had large bags under black eyes that gave no glimmer of mental activity. They were Mama, Papa and baby bear.

 Todd's mother kept hugging and kissing him on the cheek. He actually blushed. Swear to God. She had embarrassed the unembarrassable. I felt more than a twinge of jealousy. "What is my problem?," I wondered.

 Before they left, Todd pulled me aside and handed me a slip of paper.

 "Here's my phone number. Call me if you do something Rory-ish. I don't want to miss anything good."

 "Come along, Toddie" his mother called. After they left, I tried thinking of the last time my mother called me anything. She would refer to me as "him" to my father even when I was seated right next to her.

 It was eerily quiet when I slept in my dorm right that night. As far as I knew, everyone in my building had gone home for the summer. I probably wasn't supposed to be there but I steered clear of the campus police and my presence went undetected.

 I slept on Todd's bed. He had a mattress as well as a box spring. I had packed up my sheets earlier, not thinking ahead. Sleeping in an empty college dormitory is a lonely feeling and it took a while before I fell unconscious into a dream about Diane, the perfect capper to a depressing day.

 When I woke up, I realized that my clothes were all packed up. I had forgot to lay out clothes the night before and had to open up my suitcase to find something to wear. In the dorm lobby, someone from campus security stopped me.

 "What the hell are you doing? You're supposed to be gone."

 "I have to speak to a professor. I'll be out of here by noon."

For a liberal arts college that prides itself on being so forward thinking, the campus was literally littered with litter. In the rush to head home, a wide assortment of debris was left behind. Couch cushions, lamps, books, papers, jackets, pants, shoes, cardboard boxes, supermarket milk crates (Drake wouldn't like that) were all scattered about. It was as if the entire student population simultaneously had a one night stand and got the hell out of there before their partner awoke.

I got to McKensie Hall, one of the brick anchors of the campus quad and made my way to Jelinak's office. I knocked.

"There's nothing more to discuss," he yelled before opening the door, "Oh, it's you" he said.

He'd been crying. More accurately, he was still crying. He was in fact, in the <u>middle</u> of crying when I knocked on his door. His emotions abruptly shifted from "sad" or at least "emotional" to "embarrassment."

"Come in" he said quickly finding tissues to wipe his eyes, "I thought you were someone else."

Tentatively, I entered.

"Are you okay?"

"I'm fine" he snapped, "This has nothing to do with you."

I didn't actually think it had anything to do with me. To my knowledge none of my professors sit in their office crying over me. It's just that when you come across someone young or old, male or female, bawling their eyes out the natural question is "Are you okay?"

"Have a seat" he had stopped crying now. He sat across from me. He put his glasses on probably more to hide his red eyes than to see me clearly.

"I think people should mean what they say, don't you?"

I had no idea what he was referring to but as a general concept I do think people should mean what they say.

"Yes," I said.

"I was wrong to be curt with you, please forgive me."

"No problem" I replied.

I'm not sure which of us was more embarrassed. If I could have unknocked and tiptoed backwards down the hallway without him ever knowing I was there I would have.

"What can I do for you?"

I exhaled.

"I'd like to come back."

"You realize the semester is over, don't you?"

He said this with a slight smile.

"I just don't want to flunk out."

"I'm glad to hear that" he said, "We have to make sure that doesn't happen."

He stood up and with his back to me looked out the window. He had suddenly donned an authoritative air. Moments earlier, he was a man in his early 40's weeping openly and now he was clearheaded and purposeful.

"I didn't give you an 'F'" he said, "I gave you an incomplete. Let's talk to the Dean and see if you can get an incomplete in all of your classes instead of 'F's."

"What's the difference?"

"All 'F's would kill your GPA and you'd probably get kicked out. An incomplete is the academic equivalent of a do over. Let's go talk to the Dean before he leaves on his trip."

As he put on his sports jacket he asked, "What's your GPA?"

"3.1" I said. "Good, good" he said, "That helps."

He opened the door. "Oh" he said looking directly at me, "When we talk to the Dean, let's focus on the part where you had trouble dealing with your mother's death and leave out the part about getting your girlfriend pregnant."

THIRTY-SIX

Although it took me a while to figure out what I wanted to be when I grew up I knew at an early age what I didn't want to be. I didn't want to be like my Dad. I didn't want to marry a woman like my mother and the one day I went to work with my Dad was enough to convince me that I didn't want to be an accountant.

I was six years old. I was in kindergarten (I had gotten a late start) and it was during the February school break. My Mom had come down with some kind of a flu. I remember being frightened by the volatile, violent, vomiting sounds coming from her bathroom.

As my father was leaving for work, she called down to him from the top of the stairs in her bathrobe and slippers, "You're going to have to take him with you." He stood at the door staring blankly up at her raising objections in his head. Yet, he knew she was right. She was too sick to take care of me and I was too young to be left unsupervised.

He told me to pick out a toy to bring with me. I went to my room and pulled out the toy box from under my bed. It was a difficult decision and I agonized over it.

"Rory," he said sharply, "I'm going to be late."

I chose my army guy, my favorite gift from the most recent Christmas and he bundled me up for the long walk to the office. It was one of those winters that was so cold it hardly snowed and the small part of my face that was showing froze. The bulky mittens I wore made me keep dropping my army guy. Annoyed, my Dad picked it up and put it in his pocket.

"You're making me late."

We arrived at his office around 9:30. It's not easy getting all the way across town with six-year-old legs and a frozen face. As he removed my hat and unwrapped my scarf my Dad apologized to the receptionist for being late. She seemed excited to see me.

"Is this Rory?"

She had actually heard of me.

"Say hi to Mrs. Little, Rory."

I had heard of her. Around the house, my father referred to her as "Mrs. Do-Little," one of his few jokes. She was a kind woman of about thirty who wasn't stingy with the make-up brush. "You are so adorable. (These were my pre-scar days) The women from the office are going to eat you up."

She was only slightly exaggerating. On the way to my Dad's office we were stopped by one woman after another, even the men crouched down to shake my hand. I was offered candy from candy bowls and sticks of gum. Almost everyone knew my name. I was a matinee idol greeted by an adoring public.

There was one notable exception. My father's boss Mr. Gilmore or Gilman or Gilmet maybe, I can't remember which, stopped in his tracks upon seeing me.

"What's he doing here?"

"Helen's sick. She's got the flu."

"Of all days," he said, rolling his eyes. "I need to see you in my office right away."

For simplicity sake, let's call him, "Gilmore." He was about ten years younger than my Dad. He was broad shouldered and like most men bigger and more imposing than my Dad. I waved up at him and said, "Hi." Apparently, he didn't hear me as he turned and walked away.

My father ushered me quickly into his office and took off his coat and hung it up.

"Here," he said, bringing me a soda. "Behave yourself. I'll be back in a few minutes."

My father's desk was cluttered with stacks of manila folders. There was an adding machine and right behind it, a framed picture of a baby I assumed was me. On the other side, there was a picture of my mother as a young woman. On the wall, there was a family portrait that must have been taken when I was around three. I was the only one smiling not knowing any better.

I spilled my soda on the chair. I tried cleaning it up with some tissues but they disintegrated almost immediately and left the seat wet and sticky with little strands of tissue. I remembered my army guy and found it in my Dad's coat pocket. I was playing with it on the floor when he came back.

He sat down in the chair in the soda spill. He didn't seem to notice. He took his glasses off and rubbed his eyes.

"Dad?"

"Not now, Rory."

He covered his face with his hands.

"Are you okay, Daddy?"

"Not now."

Gilmore entered and stood over him.

"You know, I let the Christmas party thing go."

My Dad whispered, "I know."

"I figured people drink at Christmas parties and sometimes things get out of hand, but I can't ignore those letters."

My Dad nodded.

"For Christ sake, she even signed them."

No one said anything for a moment. Gilmore looked at my Dad then me on the floor and then back at my Dad.

"I'll write you a letter of recommendation if you need one."

I felt like crying but I didn't know why exactly. Gilmore left.

My Dad leaned back in his chair and stared at the ceiling. A minute or two later, a woman with chubby ankles came in. I was under the desk now and couldn't see her face.

"I want you to know I don't blame you Walter. Maybe I shouldn't have shown Ken those letters but they scared me."

My father didn't respond.

"I certainly didn't mean for you to get fired but I'm sure you'll land on your feet."

"I have some things to do," he said, almost forcefully. "Of course."

The chubby ankles disappeared from my sight lines. My Dad stood up. He violently overturned a cardboard box filled with manila folders. He began pulling things from desk drawers and sticking them in the box. He threw in the pictures of us. I heard the sound of glass breaking.

"We have to go now," he said. He corralled me from under the desk and put on my coat and hat and scarf. Word must have gotten out. The office which was so happy to see me an hour earlier now watched us leave in stunned silence. Tears slogged their way down Mrs. Little's make-up. "Good-bye," my Dad said softly passing her desk.

Halfway home, we stopped at a diner so my Dad could put the box down. I ordered a hot chocolate and then discovered my toy was missing.

"Dad, we have to go back. I left my army man."

"Rory," he said, "We can never go back there again."

Over hot chocolate and coffee, I cried outwardly while my father cried inwardly over what we had each lost forever.

When we finally entered our house it was around noon and my mother jumped out of bed thinking we were burglars.

"What are you doing here?" she asked.

Then she saw the box in my father's hands.

"What did you do?" she barked at me. "What did he do?" she demanded again this time from my Dad. My father said nothing as he walked outside to chop some firewood.

THIRTY-SEVEN

I had never met the Dean. He spoke to us as a group the first day of school freshman year. I remember he used the word "inspired" a lot. He urged us to become "inspired" by our surroundings and become "inspired" by our teachers. If you ask me, it wasn't a very "inspired" speech.

After that, I would see him on campus from time to time. He was famous for playing pick-up basketball on Friday afternoons with a group of students. His jump shot, never blocked out of deference, had once been renowned at one of the Ivy League schools many years ago. Now, each year, it lands less and less frequently at its desired location. Needless to say, I never played in these games and he knew neither my name nor my face.

Todd knew him, having been called into his office once or twice for disciplinary reasons. In Todd's view, this cemented their friendship. When the Dean passed through our cafeteria, Todd would stand up and wave with exaggerated gregariousness and call out loudly, "Hi, Deanie!" The Dean would look over at this extra-large man with the cherubic face, wave back feebly and continue on his way.

"Let me do the talking," Jelinak said as we sat in the Dean's outer office "I've known Leonard a long time."

Was he trying to impress me by using the Dean's first name? I said nothing which was good practice for the upcoming meeting.

"You can go in now," his secretary announced.

I followed Jelinak into the Dean's office. The Dean looked different up close. His face was lined and worn and his hair which had been streaked with gray was now a uniformed and unnatural black. Why would a dean at a college dye his hair? Isn't looking distinguished part of the job? Wouldn't a dean who had jet black hair dye his hair gray?

"Dean, this is Rory Collins. He's a sophomore."

We shook hands. There was a large bookcase, possibly for show, against the wall. I noticed on his desk, he had a miniature replica of the same statue of Colonel Philbin on his horse found in the center of campus. I also noticed that Jelinak called him "Dean" and not "Leonard."

"Dean, Rory, here lost his Mom this semester."

The Dean winced in pain.

"Oh, I am sorry to hear that. How old was she?" He said as his voice suddenly got soft. "Forty-Four."

"Was it sudden?"

"Yes, sir, her heart gave out."

I probably should have called the Dean years later when I found out the truth.

"My mistake, Leonard, she died when she shot herself in the head using the same shotgun her father used when he shot himself in front of his young children."

That would have been a memorable chat.

"What is it that I can do?" The Dean asked looking at Jelinak and not me. "You see, Dean, Rory didn't handle his mother's death very well. He's an only child. His father is quite a bit older. He was very close to his mother."

I wasn't sure where he got his information. He and I had never discussed such things. It must have been from Todd. My mind wandered now to the day Todd and Jelinak abducted me and brought me to the diner. How did that come about? Did Todd go to Jelinak out of concern for me? It seemed unlikely. Jelinak must have noticed I wasn't showing up for class. His curiosity piqued, he stopped by my dorm room where Todd and he discussed my situation and decided to take action.

The Dean cleared his throat. I better pay attention, I thought. Jelinak clasped his hands together dramatically.

"Rory, did not manage his grief."

The Dean nodded and looked at me.

"Did you know this institution provides counselors for situations like yours."

"No sir," I said truthfully.

"Rory is an introvert. He's not one to open up to a counselor or even his roommates. In fact, his roommate told me they never once discussed his mother's death."

Part of me wanted to burst out laughing. Was I really supposed to bear my soul to Todd? Share my innermost thoughts with a guy who spends two hours every day scratching his balls?

Jelinak put his hand on my shoulder.

"Rory's grief manifested itself by his complete withdrawal from society. He stopped going to class entirely. He turned down help from his friends and teachers. When his mother's heart stopped, Rory stopped along with it."

When he said this last comment about my Mom, a chill came over me. I suddenly felt like there was no one in the world more full of shit than me. I wasn't close to my mother. When she died, I didn't shed a single tear. To me, she was a mentally disturbed woman who I pitied on a good day and hated on a bad.

Jelinak wasn't describing how I felt. He was describing how I should have felt. He was describing what a normal person would feel. It was probably how he felt when his mother died. There must be something wrong with me. I started to cry and couldn't stop. No one said a word for what seemed like a long time.

The Dean turned to Jelinak in a near whisper, "What do you recommend?"

"I'm giving Rory an incomplete instead of an F. Perhaps, you could convince his other teachers to do the same. He has a B average.

He's willing to take summer school classes. He can take five classes each remaining term and still graduate on time."

"All right then, let's do that."

I wiped away my tears. The Dean shook my hand again.

"We'll get you back on track, young man."

THIRTY-EIGHT

When I was in high school I never really thought about going to college. I know that sounds dumb but it's true. I went to high school because you had to. I was actually a pretty good student. I was in honors English and honors history. (I did less well in biology and math) The thought of what came next didn't occur to me. I was like a man riding an escalator not realizing at some point I'd have to get off.

I had some vague notion that my parents went to college but they never talked about it. There was never any "do well in school so you can go to a good college" or "you need to put some money aside for college." The word never came up.

This isn't to say that college is for everyone because it isn't. There are plenty of bright people for whom the notion of sitting in a classroom is torture. They'd much rather be building something or fixing something or growing something. I was not one of those people.

It wasn't until September of my senior year when my guidance counselor Ms. Gillen asked me what colleges I was applying to that I realized I should think about the next step. I brought it up that night at dinner. "No" my mother said. This was just after the summer of Diane and she was barely speaking to me.

"But Helen, he has to do something. He'll never make a living with his hands."

My father was also aware that there was nothing I could build or fix or grow.

"He's not going anywhere."

"Helen."

"He's staying right here where I can keep an eye on him."

When I was growing up there was an old woman, Miss Nolan, who lived next door who lived alone. She had always lived alone, an old Irish maiden aunt. When I was little she was quite taken with me. She would bake me cookies from time to time and she often told my parents what a cute boy I was, that sort of thing. When I got a little older, not even a teenager but ten or eleven - Miss Nolan stopped liking me. I wasn't little and cute any more. I had committed an unforgivable act, I'd grown older.

This was how my mother was acting now. How dare I grow up? Going away to college was akin to running away from home. It was an act of betrayal. The fact that she couldn't stand me didn't seem to factor into her thought processes.

The next day, I told Ms. Gillen my parents didn't want me to go to college she was stunned. Students who weren't headed to college took shop class and woodworking and auto repair. They didn't take honors English and honors history.

"Is it about the money?," she whispered, "Because you can get financial aid."

That night after dinner, I was in the bathroom when I heard the doorbell ring. No one ever came to our house. Even Jehovah Witnesses knew better than to knock on our door. It was Ms. Gillen. She'd come to discuss my future. My parents were so surprised by this sneak attack they let her in.

I listened from the top of the stairs. It was frustrating. Both my father and Ms. Gillen were so soft spoken it was difficult to hear the conversation. For the most part, only my mother's booming declarations, "You don't know him the way I do" and "over my dead body" made their way to the second floor.

Ms. Gillen stayed for almost an hour. She was young and blonde and petite and could have passed for a college student herself. Yet, she held her ground like the regiment from Maine on Little Round Top.

After she left, my parents continued to argue.

"Why should I listen to her? She's nine years old."

I was unable to hear my father's response. That night, shortly after I'd gone to bed, my father came into my room, "This weekend, we'll look at some colleges."

My father didn't drive which created problems. For the next four weekends, we took trains in different directions to look at schools. My mother seethed. She now broadened her silent treatment to include my father. To punish me, she stopped making my school lunches.

There must be thirty colleges a reasonable distance from Addison. Some schools were ruled out immediately. Anything too big would be overwhelming. Penn and a couple of other schools were ruled out by Ms. Gillen as "beyond my scope." It was a nice way of saying, "You're not smart enough."

This left about a dozen to look at of which I liked three. Having no idea of a career, my only criteria was how the campus looked and did I feel I'd fit in there. At one place, for instance, the student body seemed too rich and too preppy to welcome the likes of me.

Philbin was the last one we saw. I liked it but not necessarily better than the little one in Philadelphia and the other little one in Ohio. I stood with my Dad under the shadow of Philbin's statue and looked around. "What do you think?" my Dad asked. "I'm not sure" I said.

I surveyed the scene once more. I noticed engraved at the base of the statue was Philbin's lifespan. Born November 20th, 1838 Died May 5th, 1910. November 20th also happens to be my birthday. It was a sign. "I'll go here," I said.

THIRTY-NINE

"Well, that's taken care of," Jelinak said as we left the Dean's office. "Leonard's really a blithe spirit even if you have to massage his ego from time to time."

I noticed he was back to calling the Dean "Leonard" now that he was out of ear shot. I guess "blithe spirit" was his way of saying the Dean was a good guy.

Afterwards, we went to the registrar and I signed up for two classes, one of which was his. I kind of had to with him standing over my shoulder. When we got back to the office, Jelinak asked what my plans were. Plans have never been my strong suit.

"Do you have a summer job?"

I guess I do need one now that he mentioned it.

"The maintenance crew is always shorthanded; would you want to work there?"

"Sure."

He walked me down to lower campus. There was a garage behind Claflin Hall I'd never noticed before even though I'd walked past it a million times. We entered. There was a red-faced man reading the sports pages.

"Hi, I'm Professor Jelinak, I'm head of the Psychology Department in the School of Fine Arts."

Professors always love to give their credentials. "I understand you have some summer jobs available."

"Hey, Keith," the red-faced man bellowed, "One of the profs is here."

Keith emerged from the back. He had to be around sixty years old. I'd never seen a guy that old named Keith before. He should have been "Gus" or "Larry." He had the name of a man half his age.

Jelinak turned on the charm.

"Good afternoon, I'm Professor Jelinak. I'm the head of the Psychology Department in the school of Fine Arts."

"Good for you. Your parents must be very proud."

Jelinak faked a laugh.

"I understand you have some summer jobs available."

"Don't tell me they cut your pay," Keith replied.

The red-faced man laughed.

Puzzled, Jelinak said, "It's not for me, it's for him."

Keith looked me over.

"He's a sophomore here at the college."

"We don't just hire anybody."

"Oh, um, of course," Jelinak said.

"Hey, kid, have you ever murdered anyone?"

"No, sir."

"All right, you got the job."

The red-faced man laughed again. Jelinak seemed baffled by the whole exchange.

"We're supposed to start at nine but things don't really get going around here until ten." "What do I wear?" I asked.

"What do you wear? Let's see, tomorrow's Tuesday that's black tie optional. What the fuck, kid, we cut grass and paint dorm rooms."

What a blithe spirit!

Jelinak and I retreated to the safety of upper campus.

"Where are you staying tonight?" He caught me off-guard. It didn't occur to me that since I'm now going to summer school I would need a place to live. God, I'm a moron. He must have noticed my blank expression.

"That settles it. You'll spend tonight at my place."

I don't know if I've mentioned it but Jelinak is short, bald, and pudgy with a hook nose. He was the kind of a guy you could lose an insult fight to only because you wouldn't know where to start. There were too many choices. Yet for all his shortcomings, he has charisma. No professor at our school has a larger or a more devoted following. He's spoken of with great reverence by students and professors alike. How does someone who looks like him have charisma? I don't know but Gorbachev has it and he has that thing on his head.

I noticed his car had a bumper sticker that reads "Commit Random Acts of Kindness." "I must be one of those random acts," I thought. He must go around helping people like me because he is an incredibly kind person. We got in and he drove like a maniac.

He lived in an old Victorian on the outskirts of town. The lawn needed cutting. There were boxes stacked up in the living room and tall bookcases half filled with books. The title "Sex and Death" caught my eye. I followed him as he weaved his way between the stacks. He stopped abruptly and faced me.

"Do you know Professor Sato? She teaches Art History. Petite Japanese woman with a cute body, she's my wife."

Don't talk to me about your wife's body, jeez. I shook my head "no." He continued into the kitchen and I followed.

He opened a bottle of wine and poured us each a glass. He had me chop lettuce while he made dinner. He was no Fitzhugh.

"She's leaving me," he said.

I kept my head down and continued to chop.

"During my office hours she comes here and packs up, hence the boxes."

He uses the word "hence" in conversation.

"That's more than enough," he said and I stopped chopping.

He asked me to set the table while he prepared the meat.

"She was my third wife, you know."

I didn't.

"She's Japanese. Her family is anyway."

He had already told me this but I acted like it was new information. My first wife was Chinese and my second wife was Korean."

This was impressive considering the area where we lived was 98% Caucasian. He poured himself another glass.

"I have a thing for Oriental women," he said. (In those days, people could use the word "Oriental" without being considered racist.) "They're supposed to be submissive but they never are. People confuse submissive with passive aggressive."

He was crying. The tears were still in his eyes but there was no mistaking them. I excused myself and went to the bathroom. When I got back my glass was filled to the top.

All through dinner, he talked about his wives. He described what they looked like and how they met. He talked about the trips they took together and the mistakes he had made. He told me what each of them were doing now. I did almost none of the talking. For dessert, we had some cookies out of a box.

After dinner, he opened another bottle of red. I was still working on my first glass when he topped me off.

"So," he said, "I understand you had quite a year with the ladies."

"Pardon?"

"Your roommate told me all about it. I'd like to hear it from you."

"There's not much to say really."

"Oh, come on, Rory, I shared with you all of my marital endeavors. The least you can do is fill me in on your activities. I thought we were friends."

I saw what was happening. He had wined me and dined me and now he wanted sex. I resisted at first but eventually I gave in. I told him everything about every woman I slept with. Actually, I told him more than everything because I made up stuff that wasn't true. I made up "firm breasts" and "thin waists." I invented moles and tattoos. You never saw a guy listening harder. I'm surprised he didn't take notes.

It occurred to me that being a psychology professor is the perfect profession for a sex fiend. Let's face it, psychology is all about sex. It's a socially acceptable way you can read about it, study it and talk about it all day long and no one thinks you're a perv. You're a respected member of the community.

When I finished he seemed sexually satisfied. He stood up a little unsteadily.

"Are you going to be okay sleeping on this couch?"

"Sure, sure."

"Good, I'll see you in the morning."

He went upstairs and I brushed my teeth and lay down on the couch feeling more ashamed of myself than ever.

FORTY

It was Gabriel who found my mother's diaries. Technically, I found them but I wouldn't have without him. It was shortly after my father died, the three of us drove down from Philadelphia. We were cleaning out his house and Gabriel was playing in my parent's bedroom, something I was forbidden to do.

Once, when I was five years old, I had a nightmare. I don't exactly remember all the details but it involved a bad man bludgeoning my father with an ax while my mother and I hid under the bed. I should have known better than to have an oedipal dream. It turned out to be the pleasant part of my evening.

I woke up crying and ran into my parents' bedroom. They weren't having sex, fortunately, or maybe I would have been the one who committed suicide instead of my mother. They were simply sleeping. In fact, they were both sound asleep which now makes me suspect my mother had taken some pills.

I had to shake her awake. "

What's happening?" she yelled and sat bolt upright.

My father turned on the light. I stood next to their bed bawling.

"I had a bad dream," I whimpered, "A bad man-"

That was as far as I got.

"Rory Hector Collins," she said pointing an accusing finger, "You know that you are not allowed in this bedroom. It's my private sanctuary. Your father is lucky I let him sleep here."

I looked over at my Dad who somewhat reluctantly nodded in agreement.

I'd like to take a quick moment to apologize for not mentioning sooner that my middle name was "Hector." Of course, if your middle name is Hector it's not the kind of thing you go around telling people. They chose that name because my father was fond of Greek mythology and my mother was fond of being cruel to me. Hector was the perfect choice.

She wasn't finished, "Go back to your room this instant and tomorrow your father and I will decide if we'll even let you stay in this house anymore."

I went to my room that instant, shocked at how ungrateful my mother was. Moments earlier, I had saved her from a maniac with an ax and this was the thanks I got.

This was the first time I'd been in her bedroom since. There was wallpaper coming off parts of the wall. I had to laugh because that summer when she and I wallpapered the whole house, we did every room except her bedroom. I was still not allowed in even for that.

Occasionally, when I was younger I'd fantasize about my mother in her bedroom having a heart attack and needing CPR or choking on a sandwich and pleading for me to administer the Heimlich. In those day dreams, I'd stand at the threshold shrugging, "Sorry but forbidden is forbidden."

The bed frame, the two dressers and the stand alone mirror all looked old. Not old in a cool, antique way, old in a "they should have thrown this stuff out" way. We were planning a yard sale and I knew these things wouldn't bring much but when you're on a teacher's salary and your wife's in school you get what you can.

Between the closet and the bedroom there was a rope dangling from the ceiling. Gabriel was swatting at it with the plastic sword he always carried around with him. He was in a medieval phase, a history buff just like his Dad. He kept smacking the rope from side to side slaying an invisible dragon. I hadn't been in that room for twenty years. I'd forgotten all about that rope.

The rope hung from a trap door in the ceiling. I pulled it down to reveal a handful of stairs. I tried to boost myself up but I wasn't strong enough. After three tries, I gave up and went to the kitchen for the step ladder. Using the ladder I was able to reach the steps from the ceiling and climb inside the cramped attic space.

The smell of must and dust was powerful as was the heat. I began to perspire at once. I looked from side to side. I was surrounded by pink insulation and one box, one medium sized cardboard box. On all fours, I opened the box. It was filled with her notebooks. They were smaller than I remembered. They were arranged vertically as opposed to one on top of the other. I flipped through the first one, seeing my mother's handwriting for the first time in several years.

These were not the leather bound journals of Major then Colonel Philbin which historians peruse to this day. These were shabby loose leaf notebooks that cost less than fifty cents apiece.

Long ago, someone decided that when a man jots down his thoughts each day it's in a "journal" and when a woman does it it's in a "diary." Thus, Lewis and Clark kept a journal. Anne Frank, a historical figure in her own right, kept a diary. Shouldn't the distinction be based on content instead of gender? If Colonel Philbin wrote passages like "I do so have a crush on Bobby Lee. My heart is all aflutter whenever he enters the mess tent", wouldn't they have to call it a diary then?

With some difficulty, I brought the box downstairs. The attic smell was too much to bear.

"What's in the box, Daddy? Candy?"

You have to love a five-year-old's mind. You find a box hidden in an attic, what else could be inside? This was his version of buried treasure.

"Sorry to disappoint you, Gabriel, no candy just some notebooks."

Given my father's feeble condition I don't think he could have climbed into the attic and crawled to the box. My mother must have used the stepladder and stored the notebooks one by one. My Dad probably never knew they were there.

I sat on the bed and began to read. They were filed chronologically oldest to newest. The early entries were long, pointless ramblings about the weather, broken appliances and what she had had for breakfast and lunch. Her prose was sparse and repetitive. Some days seemed to be near carbon copies of others. It appeared that almost nothing happened day after day year after year. I was entranced.

Many of the passages were long, unfair rants about my father. Like this one, "I hate Walter. I don't believe that I ever loved him. I married him because he loved me. He's old and foolish to look at. He has gray hair in his ears. When he left for work today I thought about doing it." That one kind of jumped out at me.

It was obvious the "it" didn't mean sex but I didn't know what she meant by it. Was she thinking about leaving my father? I thought for a moment that these notebooks were too private. I shouldn't know the intimate details of my parent's marriage. It really wasn't any of my business. I kept going.

This one stunned me.

"It's almost George's birthday. I love him so much."

For a split second, I thought my mother was having an affair with some guy named George. She did say she hated my father. Then I read this, "George and I used to play Hide N'Seek indoors on rainy days like these" and I remembered her dead brother was named George. She never spoke of him and yet, here were long passages describing the games they played together and how his freckles came out every summer.

"Daddy, you said we could have a sword fight."

"We will Gabriel, just give Daddy another minute." I spotted my name for the first time. "Rory made me want to do it today."

I read at a frenzied pace. "Daddy, you promised."

"We'll go outside and have a sword fight in just a minute, Gabriel."

What was the "it" she spoke of? I heard the sound of footsteps coming up the stairs.

"Hey, how come I'm doing all the work?"

FORTY-ONE

It was early when I slipped out of Jelinak's house. I wanted to avoid the embarrassment of seeing him in the morning, his embarrassment, not mine. A paperboy rode past me on his bike and gave me a look. What did that mean? Maybe he's just not used to someone who's not female and not Asian leaving Jelinak's house.

During the war, Philbin and his superiors would meet in a tent late at night and drink coffee and assess their troops' provisions and morale and map out a battle strategy. I decided to stop at a coffee shop and do the same for myself.

I sat staring out the window. I actually began smiling. I had my identity back. For a while, I'd been a "father-to-be" then simply a "boyfriend" then a "supermarket employee" and then suddenly "nothing." I'd finally regained a little something. I was a "college student" once again. True, I had no place to live but I at least I had something to say when someone asked, "So what do you do?"

"Hey, kid," I looked up. The café owner said, "We need that table."

I walked thinking I was walking aimlessly until I realized I was headed somewhere. I'm a creature of habit. I like the familiar. I knocked on Fitzhugh's door. After a few seconds, a woman asked, "Who is it?" It took me so long to respond she probably thought I was lying. "My name is Rory Collins. I'm an old friend of Mr. Fitzhugh's."

Did Fitzhugh have a girlfriend? I'd never heard him speak of one. Nor did he strike me as gay. He appeared to be one of those rare people who seemed impervious to both sex and beauty. Once when watching the news channel, a gorgeous anchorwoman came on the air and I made a comment pointing out that fact. He seemed almost puzzled.

I had two theories. One, his only concerns were of a global nature. Sex is a personal, individual desire. His desires were for racial harmony and world peace. He was a saintly figure who cared little for himself but cared deeply that the world become a better place.

That was one theory. The other theory was simply that for him food had become a substitute for sex. The mincing, the basting and the marinating were all part of the foreplay leading up to the meal which for him signified consummation.

In any event, a moment later, Fitzhugh opened the door.

"Get in here," he said, pulling me in quickly and shutting it.

"Did anyone seeing you coming here?"

"I don't think so."

"Are you sure?" I shrugged, "I didn't see anyone. What's going on?"

"They're watching me."

"Who?"

"FBI, most likely. I got two hang-ups when I answered the phone in the past week."

I nodded and looked around for a woman.

"I heard a woman."

"That was me," Fitzhugh said suddenly using that same feminine voice I heard in the hallway. "I didn't know who was there," he said, still in the falsetto and beginning to creep me out, "I didn't want to take any chances."

"Come on in" he said, finally in his own voice and we entered the living room. It was as disgusting as ever with newspapers strewn about on the couch and floor and plates with remnants of meals that didn't appear recent. The biggest change was that the windows were taped up with cardboard boxes.

"What's all this?" I asked.

"It's so they can't look in on me. The other day, there was a guy in a phone company uniform looking in from that pole, right there. There's no doubt he was FBI. Then, yesterday morning at the supermarket, just after I put a jar of black olives in my cart, this Republican looking guy put one in his cart. What are the odds of two guys buying black olives at the same time?"

I didn't know.

"Then he was in line behind me at the checkout. They're letting me know they're keeping an eye on me."

"Wow," I said when what I really wanted to say was "Huh?" Why would the FBI care about Fitzhugh? I mean sure he hated the government having lost his job and all but he wasn't in here making bombs. He was in here making pirogues.

"What can I do for you?" I explained my situation and how I needed a place for the summer. "Sure, sure," he said when I finished.

"I can't pay you for a couple of weeks."

"You're good for it," he said. "I'm making waffles do you want some?"

"I gotta get to work," I said.

I moved towards the bedroom when he stopped me.

"Thanks for saying you were a friend of mine."

I was confused.

"At the doorway, when you knocked."

"Oh," I said. "It takes a lot of courage to admit that publicly. It could be dangerous."

"I didn't admit it publicly," I thought. I said it in the privacy of his hallway.

"Sure, sure," I said.

I peeked in my old bedroom. Mary Ann had left the mattress that Todd stole behind. I was an army on the move. I was capturing the high ground. I was back in school. I had a place to live, a summer job and a mattress to sleep on. I was on my way of achieving my life-long goal of becoming normal.

I thanked Fitzhugh and left for my first day of work. I was upbeat and for a few minutes, I savored my positive mood. Yet, there was still a missing piece. I knew I still loved Mary Ann but it occurred to me that I also loved Karen. You can love two people at once. Don't parents love multiple children? Can't you love pizza and ice cream? I decided to tell Karen how I felt. (I'd leave out the part about Mary Ann, of course) I didn't have her phone number but I knew her hometown. It was probably listed, right? How many Karen Crespis can there be in Borden, Pennsylvania?

I just didn't know exactly how to do it. I didn't want to just blurt it out the way most men do, drunkenly in a moment of passion. Men who say, "I love you" when what they really mean is "I love sex." I had made my decision soberly in broad daylight.

I resolved to call her but the idea of calling her up and telling her over the phone seemed so unsatisfying. The mass escape from the supermarket had been so dramatic. This was so bland, so ordinary.

I had never said "I love you" to anyone, not even to Mary Ann, not to my father and certainly not to my mother. It couldn't be done over the phone. It needed to be said face to face and it needed to be memorable. "Flair" was the word my mind retrieved like someone bobbing apples. It needed to be done with a certain flair. It wasn't until I was halfway across upper campus that the idea came to me.

FORTY-TWO

Colonel Philbin died at the Bradford Hotel (also no longer with us) in downtown Hillcrest in the middle of Sunday dinner with his "secretary." Secretary was a euphemism. He would choose a pretty immigrant girl from among his factory workers to be his concubine, tire of her and then find another.

Minutes before he died, Philbin and the young woman, whose name is lost to history, were in his hotel room having sex. Such behavior was scandalous at the time but Philbin was the most powerful man in town and no one dared challenge "The Colonel", the title he preferred to "former slave owner" and "employer of small children."

It's a shame he didn't die during sex. In his journals, Philbin claimed he wished he had died as a soldier in the "center of the action" or "amid the tumult" as he liked to say. It's doubtful he really meant this because the post-war years were quite good to him but death during sex would have suited him. The Colonel could have made one final call to arms (and legs). He could have sent his troops into the breach one last time. The handless man could have succumbed after a glorious, farewell handjob. Of course, I've always been the sentimental sort.

Instead, Philbin collapsed at the table in the crowded dining room of an apparent heart attack. Dr. Wakefield, a respected albeit palsied local doctor was summoned and he worked on the body as the other restaurant patrons gathered around. During the commotion, his young secretary slipped out the side door and disappeared. Wakefield's efforts proved fruitless and Philbin was pronounced dead at seventy-two, a good long life for the age.

My father's death was less dramatic, less sudden and less of a public spectacle. We were in his hospital room at the end, even Gabriel. Was it dumb to let a five-year-old watch his grandfather die? Probably but we had nowhere to leave him this far from home. As silly as it sounds, Gabriel kept insisting on seeing the dying man. When one of us would sit with him in the cafeteria he'd say over and over, "I want to see Grandpa." Eventually, we gave in. He doesn't seem traumatized.

Gabriel and I visited my father three months earlier after I came home to find this message on our answering machine, "I have cancer, beep." My Dad was never one for small talk. One nice thing about being a teacher is you have summers off so Gabriel and I drove down the following week.

The three of us bonded at the woodpile. Gabriel and my father sat on the stump while I chopped some firewood. The whole time I suspected, correctly as it turned out, that by the time the weather turned cold my father wouldn't be around to use it.

While I worked, Gabriel watched me and my father watched him. He seemed to take delight in everything Gabriel did. Did he look at me the same way when I was that age? If so, it's a memory I must have repressed.

That night for dinner, I made Fitzhugh's Chicken Masala.

"Where did you learn to cook?" My Dad asked.

Parents are always amazed when their children learn something outside of their purview. "It's just something I picked up."

It was dinner for three once again and there was little conversation while we ate. Even Gabriel who normally chatters away seemed worn out from chopping wood. It was the same table in the same kitchen in the same house yet the silence was different. It's a funny how silence works, it can be tension or it can be serenity all without saying a word.

That night after dinner, after Gabriel had had his bath and gone to bed, my father and I sat in the living room and watched an old movie the way we used to. Of course, this time we watched without my mother's running commentary.

Halfway through the movie I got this sudden voice in my head daring me to tell my Dad I loved him.

"Go on, he's dying of cancer."

"I don't want to" another voice replied.

"Do it."

"That's not our way," I argued back defensively.

I believe that actions say "I love you" far better than mere words. Visiting my Dad, chopping wood for him, making him dinner, these things said, "I love you." A philandering, abusive husband might tell his wife "I love you" again and again but his actions belie his words. I didn't say it.

Two months later, we all drove down to Philadelphia for the final visit. While Gabriel slept, my wife and I joked about the term "death bed." "What kind of a store sells a 'death bed'? "Why would anyone buy one?" When we arrived at my Dad's hospital room the joking stopped and a wave of guilt washed over me.

My Dad, never a big man, was now Lilliputian. His skin, waxen and yellow, was draped like a towel over his bony frame. Tubes were coming in and out of him and a bit of drool leaked continuously from his mouth even though his eyes were open and alert.

That night, my eyes were just as open as I lay awake in our motel room. Was I here because I loved him or because I was supposed to love him? Did I come out of love or duty or some societal convention? Once you become a parent, you become a little more forgiving of your own parents because you hope your child will forgive your shortcomings.

The next day, we let Gabriel see him and his eyes registered a flicker of a smile. For a few hours, he seemed to rally and I wondered aloud if he would be strong enough to come home. We spent the rest of the week sitting around his bed. How I wished we had something to reminisce about.

By Friday, he had slipped into a coma. That didn't stop Gabriel from conversing with him, "Grandpa when you wake up, do you want to play with me?"

The nurse came in periodically to check his vital signs. Finally, she looked at me and said softly, "It won't be long now." The three of us stood, surrounding him, holding hands. I leaned over and whispered into his ear, "I love you." Minutes later, he took one last, shuddering breath. I asked my wife, "Did that count?"

FORTY-THREE

I made it from Fitzhugh's place (now my place too, I guess) to my new job at nine. I know he said things didn't really get going until ten but I wanted to make a good impression. There was no one there at nine. The garage door Jelinak and I had walked through the day before was pulled down. I knocked and got no response. I went around back and peeked in the window and saw nothing.

I was glad I was the first one there. It showed initiative. By nine-thirty, I was getting anxious, "Where the hell was everybody?" By nine-fifty, I was getting angry, "Where the hell was everybody?" At ten past ten, I was gripped by anxiety. Did I show up at the wrong place? Is everybody else off painting dorm rooms or cutting grass and wondering where the hell I was?

At ten-fifteen, I breathed a sigh of relief when I saw the red-faced man come shuffling down the hill, "You're early, kid." He unlocked and pulled up the garage door. His name turned out to be "Steve."

A few minutes later, Keith showed up with a newspaper under tucked under his arm. He nodded, "Hello" then basically ignored me. Keith and Steve divided up the paper like an old married couple. They each had a section and when they finished, they switched.

While this was going on, three or four guys my age and twice my size showed up. They were all football players. Colleges love to give football players job like these. I don't have much in the way of pecs and delts and lats and they didn't acknowledge me until I mentioned to one of them that Todd was my roommate. That got his attention.

"Hey, this guy lives with Todd."

191

The other two football players cracked up at this news and smacked each other playfully. Some of those punches looked like they hurt. Why do they do that?

One of the football players got a curious look on his face.

"Wait, you're not the guy who knocked up all those chicks are you?"

First of all, I would never use the word "chick." "Chick" was one of those words like "booze" or "dame" that doesn't belong our generation. It's a word you hear from people my parents' age or in old movies.

Yet, for some reason, it's a word that attracts attention and as soon as he said it all of the players were looking my way. He had caught me off-guard and I stammered for a moment implicating myself by the second.

"Oh, man," he said, "This is the guy who knocked up like four chicks." (There's that word again)

"It was only two," I said, "And one didn't really count."

This broke them up and they were suddenly too busy smacking each other's pecs and delts to hear my explanation.

For the next twenty minutes or so they gaped and snickered and marveled that the one they had heard so much about was actually in their midst. Finally, around ten-forty-five, Keith folded his newspaper.

"All right," he said, calling us over, "C'mon."

We all gathered around.

"Let's get down to business. Who's going to get coffee?"

The football players looked around.

"I will" I said.

On my way out the door I heard someone yell, "Don't get anyone pregnant while you're gone."

A little after eleven, I was back with the coffee.

"He brought some extra sugars," Keith announced, "We're going to have to send him for coffee every day. Not everybody can handle the responsibility."

Everyone turned to one of the football players and laughed at a joke I wasn't privy to.

We loaded some paint cans and brushes and a tarp onto a couple of golf carts. They were similar to regular golf carts except they had flat beds in the back like a pick-up truck. We rode to upper campus with Keith and Steve, Steve driving with coffee in one hand and the steering wheel in the other.

We entered a dorm room on the first floor, moved some furniture and put a tarp down on the carpet. Keith checked his watch, "It's almost twelve, who's going to get lunch?" "

I will" I said.

"I love this kid. He's a go-getter."

When I came back, we sat on the floor against the wall on top of the clear plastic tarp and ate our sandwiches. "I want to hear some Todd stories," a football player declared looking at me. I got the feeling Todd was even more of a legend than I was. I finished chewing.

"All right" I said accepting the challenge.

My favorite Todd story was the one that made Karen laugh the hardest. It was from first semester freshman year. Todd had already spent one year at a big time school with a real football team and had been bounced out for reasons I never uncovered. He started over again at Philbin with a cache of knowledge not normally possessed by an incoming freshman.

After the semester got under way, Todd would scan the bulletin board in our dorm lobby, find out where the gay and lesbian clubs were holding their events and show up with a case of beer. Todd was not gay, mind you, he just liked watching lesbians dance. These events were mostly attended by women. There weren't too many openly gay guys in those days and even the most obvious types didn't dare risk the exposure but Todd would go. He'd sit in the corner and drink his beer and watch the lesbians dance. If a gay guy approached Todd would snarl at him and he would scamper away. Todd could be quite scary when he wanted to be.

The lesbians didn't know what to make of him. Some suspected he was a creep while others wondered if he was gay and was dipping his toe in the water. In any event, they left him alone and went about their business. Todd attended three such mixers without incident.

It was during the fourth one, the one right before Christmas that Todd came out of his shell. He got there early sat in his usual spot and according to his calculations drank close to a case of beer. That night, there was one particularly gorgeous lesbian couple that Todd could not stop leering at. These two women were gyrating to the music and swishing their bodies and driving Todd crazy.

Finally, after a slow song came on, the two began slow dancing and then making out. This was too much for Todd to bear. He put his beer down, stood up and staggered towards the dance floor. The two women with their eyes closed and the music blasting didn't see or hear him coming. Todd leaned in and joined his tongue to theirs.

As you can imagine, his tongue wasn't welcome. The women shrieked and one began kicking Todd in the shins. The music stopped, an angry Sapphic mob gathered and the campus police were summoned. That Monday, Todd had his first meeting with the Dean (Leonard!) and was banned from all future gay and lesbian events.

The football players enjoyed this story immensely, hitting and slapping each other in delight. Even Keith and Steve who I didn't know were listening cracked up.

"I gotta meet this guy," Keith said.

The funny thing is when Todd told me that story later that night as we lay in our beds, I didn't believe him. I hadn't known Todd very long and as he told me I listened and silently scoffed, "No one would do such a thing."

As time went on, I realized how mistaken I was. Todd lived a life that needed no embellishment.

I remember how hard Karen laughed when I told her that story. She was giving me a ride home from the supermarket and I don't remember why I told it. The image of her, bent over the steering wheel wiping away happy tears is seared into my brain. She has a big, raucous laugh that comes from deep inside. She laughs like a man, like a sailor on leave with his buddies. I knew that if I were ever to hear that laugh again that my plan had better work.

FORTY-FOUR

It was a simple idea, really. I didn't mean to oversell it. It was a sign, that's all. I would make a giant "I Love You" sign or more accurately, a giant "I Love You, Karen" sign. She would wake up on Saturday morning and find a giant sign stretched across her front lawn proclaiming my love for her. What woman wouldn't want that?

I don't mean to imply that all women want my love but you get the point. This would be the story we'd tell our grandchildren. We wouldn't tell them about how we met in a bathroom and had sex on the toilet. We'd skip the part where she played amateur pimp bringing me one hideous woman after another to fornicate with. This would be the romance that we've never had.

I spent the rest of the week with the details percolating in my head. When half of your day is spent in a room by yourself painting a blank wall you have plenty of time to figure out every step of your preposterous schemes.

I needed a long roll of white paper that I could spread out and then roll up again. What then? Should the sign be painted or colored in with magic marker? I settled on spray paint. It was my mother's weapon of choice after all. I'd write it out in magic marker and then fill it in with spray paint.

Then what? The sign would have to be hung. I'd need some string or twine. I'd have to punch two holes in either end then use the twine to tie it between two trees. Everyone has trees in their yard. I'd need a hammer and two nails. I'd tie the string to the trees and wrap it around the nail at each end.

I'd have to leave early before dawn. Would the bus leave that early? Probably not. Not on a Saturday. I'd have to go the night before. I'd check into a motel in Borden. I'd wake up before dawn. I'd work quietly in the dark the way my mother did…twice.

By the time the sun came up, the sign would be hung and I'd be standing next to it. Her mother or father or little sister might see it first. What would they think? They'd get a kick out of it, wouldn't they? It would be like a scene from a movie. Doesn't everyone love young love?

On my way home from work on Thursday I went to the hardware store in preparation for my upcoming mission. I procured a roll of white paper, a hammer and some nails. They had string but no twine. At the pharmacy, I picked up magic markers and a hole-puncher. I even found a bus schedule. I had everything I needed to make the operation successful.

Friday night, I snatched Fitzhugh's white pages and closed the door in my bedroom. I discovered there were two Crespis living in Borden, one the home of Vincent and one the home of William. Was her Dad "Vinny" or "Bill"? I don't think she ever said.

I decided to try Vincent first. If Karen answered I'd hang up. I shook the nervousness out of my fingers and dialed. It rang four times and then Vinny answered.

"Hello, is Karen there?"

"Just a minute."

I hung up. I had all the information I needed. Karen Crespi lived at 118 Moreland Rd in Borden, Pennsylvania.

I slipped out of my room, switched the white pages for the yellow pages and returned. I made a reservation at a motel in Borden, put together and overnight bag and gathered my art supplies. "See you tomorrow," I said to Fitzhugh leaving him stoned and perplexed on the couch. I took a bus to Borden. I bought a map of the streets at a gas station and got directions to the motel.

It was more of a robust walk then I imagined and when I got to the motel it was close to ten. On the way, I thought about turning back and going home and forgetting the whole thing. "No, I am tired of being passive. I need to do this to win Karen back." I kept going.

The kid behind the counter was about my age. He looked as though he'd made a few bad choices in his life too.

"Could I get a wake-up call for four a.m.?"

He shook his head, "I'll probably be sleeping. You better set the alarm in your room."

I found my room, unfurled the roll of white paper and began making the sign. I worked slowly and meticulously. The smell from the spray can was starting to make me nauseous. By the time I got to the "y" I had to stop. I opened the door to let some cool air in. I lay down on the floor and felt dizzy. After a little while, I crawled to the bathroom and lay with my cheek against the tile. I took in long, slow deep breaths.

"I've got to finish, I've got to finish," I said over and over to myself. My head hurt but I crawled back to my spray can. I completed the message one letter at a time. After each one, I went to the door and breathed in the night air. I finally finished, then, suddenly realized I hadn't thought to bring scissors. "What is wrong with me?" I punched two holes with the hole-puncher and then I tore it carefully but unevenly with my hands.

It was 1:57 according to the clock radio in the room when I set the alarm and went to bed with a head and stomachache. I had a dream about Diane for the first time in several weeks. When I woke up, the clock read 9:23.

FORTY-FIVE

I checked and rechecked the alarm. It read 4:00. I had a vague, distant recollection of it going off. Did I reach over and shut it off and keep sleeping? I couldn't be sure. What I was sure about was that I couldn't put up my sign today. It would be a Sunday morning not a Saturday morning when I proclaimed to the world my love for Karen Crespi.

Cursing myself, I showered and got dressed. I went down to the office and paid for another night. This left me with just over five dollars that would have to hold me not only the rest of the day but the rest of the week.

I needed something to eat but I was afraid to leave my hotel room. What if Karen saw me? It's not as farfetched as it sounds. Borden is a small town. What if she was driving to work or to the mall and spotted me walking down the street? Then what? She'd pull over and want to know what the hell I was doing. My big romantic plans would be foiled.

I was still feeling a little wobbly. I had to get something to eat. I ran and fast walked to a market a few blocks away. I got two bananas and a small carton of orange juice. I ran and fast walked back.

I had a long day ahead of me. I found an old movie on television and slowly ate one of my bananas. I'd seen the movie before. It was a black and white comedy I'd watched with my parents about a love triangle and a jewelry heist and a case of mistaken identity. I hadn't enjoyed it then and I didn't enjoy it now.

In fairness, I was too angry at myself to enjoy anything. After all those years of watching old movies in the same room with someone

202 – BRIAN KILEY

who hated me, here I was again, only this time it was me who hated me.

I ate my other banana. I still had hours to go. I decided to call Fitzhugh and let him know I wasn't coming home that night. I don't know why. If I were staying over at Karen's I wouldn't call. I guess I just needed some human contact.

I found a pay phone. "Rick" (he had a first name and it was "Rick")

"It's Rory."

"Hey, man, are you all right?"

"Yeah, yeah, I'm fine. I'm just letting you know I'm not coming home tonight."

"Did you get arrested?"

Why would he think that?

"No."

"Oh, I have some friends who are at the protest today. They might get arrested."

I was too embarrassed to ask what protest. Was there something big going on today? The channel that showed the old movie didn't mention anything.

"I was supposed to go," he said, "But I ate some onions yesterday that were kinda funky and I had a rough night."

"That's too bad, see you tomorrow."

"Yeah, rock on and if anyone from the FBI is listening in, you're a fascist pig who has no respect for the Constitution."

And with that, he hung up.

Fitzhugh and I may have lived in the same apartment but we lived in two totally different worlds. He lived in a world where people railed against war and injustice and nuclear power. I lived in a world where men tried to win over women by making huge spray-painted banners. He wanted peace and I wanted love and the two were incompatible.

I was still hungry and I ran and fast walked back to the market. With only about four dollars left, I bought three bags of peanuts, a cheese stick and a little box of raisins for dessert. I could always drink water from the tap.

When I got back, a cowboy movie was just starting. Halfway through, I started to get scared. Was this dumb? What if Karen hates the idea? Mary Ann would appreciate a big, romantic gesture but I wasn't sure Karen would. What if she laughs at me? What if she gets mad for embarrassing her in front of her family and her neighbors?

Part of my problem is I don't live in the present. I was a history major and a history buff and I eventually became a history teacher. I'm like a man who walks down the road not looking forward to what's ahead but walking backwards with his eyes on the past. I wanted to create a past that Karen and I could look back on fondly.

I went to bed early, around nine-thirty, popping up every few minutes to check the time. The night before Gettysburg, Philbin barely slept. He pow-wowed with his superiors 'til midnight, then checked his sentries and wrote in his journal. The Army of the Potomac held the higher ground but he was confident they could be dislodged. He envisioned a path to Washington that would end the war. He would be a hero and a founding father of the burgeoning Confederacy. He was well aware this was to be his seminal moment and I was well aware the next day would be mine.

The alarm clock went off at four. I bolted out of bed having learned my lesson. Someone stirred in the next room, cursing my name no doubt. Love hurts. I showered and shaved and tried to look presentable. I grabbed the sign, my overnight bag and the bag with my supplies and made my move.

It wasn't too dark. It was pre-dawn, the morning equivalent of twilight. I walked quickly and my excitement grew as I neared her house. What if her parents called the cops? Why would they? What if Karen has found a new boyfriend? Already? What if they're mad that I hurt their trees? What? I admit I was a little punchy from lack of sleep.

It was close to five when I arrived at 118 Moreland. It was a modest Cape Cod, all white. There was only one tree in her yard, a large unwieldy oak. "Fuck," I thought. I realized I'd have to tie one side to the lamppost and one to the oak. It would be cockeyed, facing the house at an angle rather than straight on as I'd envisioned. It would have to be good enough.

I got to work. I tied the string to the lamppost, broke it off with my teeth and tied a knot. I hammered a nail as gently as I could into the tree then tied the string on that side. The whole process took only about seven minutes. It was still pretty dark. I could have slept another hour. I sat against the tree and closed my eyes.

I awoke when I heard a door banging. The sun was up. A man stood behind a screen door peering at me and my sign. He was older than I expected, close to seventy. Then again, my father was eighteen years older than my mother. Some people have old Dads.

He disappeared into the house which I now noticed was light blue and not white. "Karen…Karen, could you come out here?" he called.

There was laughter in his voice. Next door, a guy about forty in golf clothes and carrying a golf bag stood in his driveway staring at my sign. I stood in front of it, nervous energy coursing through my veins.

Moments later, a woman, at least sixty-five, came out of the house modestly clutching her bathrobe around the neck. She looked puzzled. The man stood back behind the screen with a sly smile on his face. I got a sudden bad feeling.

"Young man," she said kindly, "I think you've got the wrong Karen."

I turned and ran through the sign like a marathon runner reaching the finish line only I wasn't finished. I had just started. I ran as long and as far as I could.

FORTY-SIX

For my father's funeral I was at the church at 8:30. I wasn't taking any chances. I sat in a mostly dark church all alone. I knelt on that kneeling thing for a minute or so but didn't know what to say so I just sat in the pew. Father Barrett spotted me from the sacristy and came over while still wearing his black-walking-around-clothes with the Roman collar.

"You're here early," he said.

I shrugged, "I didn't want what happened last time to happen again."

He didn't seemed to know what I was referring to. It's funny how one person's traumatic event won't even register as a blip on someone else's radar screen.

At about ten of, some of the other mourners began to trickle in. My Dad had been a resident of Addison for over thirty years. He worked at an insurance company in town for sixteen years and had his own accounting firm for another fifteen. As a result, over a dozen people showed up for his funeral.

I recognized one of them as Mrs. Little. She was heavier and grayer and wore more make-up than the corpse. She sat with two women with closely cropped hair who were even heavier than she was. Karen came in just before it started. Mary Ann showed up about five minutes late with Gabriel who had never been to church before and had no concept of church etiquette.

"I'm not going to die," he proclaimed loudly halfway through the mass. He had figured out there was a guy in the box and he didn't want any part of it. I'm with him.

Barrett's eulogy for my father was just as bad as I always imagined as the one he did for my mother. He spoke mostly about God and the after-life and very little about my father. My Dad was a man of few words and people had just as few about him.

I didn't know any of the pallbearers except for Mr. Haus who owned the funeral home. I assumed they worked for him. They had gray or white hair and each maintained a grim countenance. It was one of those jobs that's only prerequisite seemed to be keeping a straight face. As long as you can avoid getting the giggles you won't get fired. I'm sure it's harder than it seems.

I stood next the hearse as they loaded my Dad's body inside thanking people for coming. Karen sidled up to me, "There is someone you should meet."

I turned to see the two women who'd been sitting with Mrs. Little; one with a square head and a square body, the other pear-shaped holding a cane. The square woman took my hand and gave it a mighty shake.

"Hi, I'm Beverly. I'm the woman who got your father fired," she said with a broad smile. My only response was a confused look.

"Your father and I had a good laugh about it the last time I saw him."

I couldn't picture my father having a good laugh with anyone.

"I met you once. You came to the office with your father. You must have been about five."

It dawned on me that it was her ankles I stared at under my father's desk the day he lost his job. "Six," I said.

"You remember?"

I nodded. "Why did he get fired?"

She chuckled and looked over at the pear with the cane. "We could laugh about it because it turned out for the best. Your father told me how much he preferred being his own boss." She still hadn't answered my question.

Karen and I waited patiently. The square woman got the hint.

"So anyway," she said, "We were at the Christmas party one year. Your father didn't usually come to the Christmas party. This was his first and only time."

Mary Ann, holding Gabriel in her arms, began eavesdropping.

"She brought your mother with him. Your mother was a very attractive woman in her day." "Thank you," I said although I'm not sure why.

"I met your mother at the coat check as we first walked in. She had on this bright red dress." The square turned to the pear, "Do you remember that red dress?"

"Oh, yeah" said the pear and the two of them smiled conspiratorially.

"Anyway, we met your mother when we first walked in and you could tell he was very proud of her. She really looked stunning in that red dress with that beautiful auburn hair."

The human pear concurred with a little too much zeal. It suddenly occurred to me that these were two old lesbians, two elderly lesbians who were ogling my dead mother. It made me uncomfortable. I'd like to think I'd be just as uncomfortable if they had been two creepy, old men.

"So, it was a typical office Christmas party, dinner, dancing…a few people got sloshed."

She paused occasionally for no reason. I had nothing to add.

"Well, I like to dance and Danny here", she gestured to Danny (Danny?) "Has a bad wheel." Danny held up her cane as evidence.

"Excuse me," Mr. Haus interrupted, "Father Barrett will be ready shortly."

"Thank you," I said and turned back to hear the rest of the story.

Squarehead continued, "As the night wore on, I danced with every guy in the office, every guy except your Dad." She took another one of her long pauses. Was she trying to build dramatic tension? "Towards the end of the night, I noticed your father sitting by himself. Your mother must have been in the ladies' room so I went over and said,

'Walter, come dance with me'. He said, 'I'm not much of a dancer' but I pulled him out on the dance floor anyway and he was right, he wasn't much of a dancer."

Karen chuckled and the pear giggled.

"But that was all right because we weren't in a dance contest. So we're dancing away…"

She shimmied a little to give me a visual. Mary Ann caught my eye and cringed.

"While we're dancing, your mother comes back from the ladies room…"

She could have stopped right there. I knew what was coming was not going to be good.

"So the music is playing and we're dancing when all of a sudden I hear a shriek. I look over and your mother's face is as red as her dress and she screams, 'Stay away from my husband!'"

I was right, this wasn't good.

She took an extra, long pause, "Now I'm a lesbian…"

"What?" said her partner in exaggerated surprise. Karen suppressed a smile.

"It's true," said Beverly.

Lesbians, of course, come in all shapes and sizes and you can't always tell. With Beverly, you can tell. Astronauts aboard the Space Shuttle can spot the Great Wall of China and Beverly's lesbianism.

"No offense, but I was about as interested in your father as I was in a bowl of dirt."

She patted my arm reassuringly. I braced myself for what came next.

"So your mother grabs a center piece off one of the tables and smashes it on the dance floor." Mary Ann gasped and a sleepy Gabriel squirmed.

"She picks up two more and smashes those. Your father is pleading, 'Please, Helen, stop.' He rushes over to her and they finally stop the music but she wasn't done. She begins snatching ashtrays off the tables and flinging them at me boomerang style."

She flicked her wrist to demonstrate.

"One missed me by about that much," she said, holding two chubby fingers a millimeter apart.

Later, Mary Ann told me she thought that Beverly was exaggerating but I don't think she was. There was no need to exaggerate when it came to my mother. The facts always strained credulity. If anything, I learned when telling a story about my mother to downplay the events to make the story more plausible.

"Finally, your father was able to hustle her out of there. They left without their coats. They must have been freezing on the way home."

Both Karen and Mary Ann avoided making eye contact with me. I wasn't sure how to respond.

"That's funny," I said softly. Why did I say that?

"Everybody liked Walter including Ken who decided not to fire your Dad after making him promise never to bring your mother to another one of the parties. So, we thought that was the end of it, but no. I started getting these letters at work calling me "a slut" and all these other names."

I'll say one thing for my Mom, she was consistent.

"Luckily, your mother didn't know my last name or where I lived but once a week or so I'd get another letter addressed to Beverly, care of Addison Insurance. They became more and more threatening, all about what she was going to do to me. I was quite shaken up one day when Ken came in my office and I showed him the letter. He hit the ceiling. That was the day you came to work with your Dad."

Haus came over again, "Fr. Barrett is ready now."

Barrett came down the church steps wearing a long, black coat with his white collar peeking out.

"I'm very sorry," I said to Beverly.

I meant I was sorry about my mother but she took it to mean "sorry that I had to go." I thanked Beverly and Danny for coming and we shared another hearty handshake. I got into the car first in line behind the hearse. Karen, Mary Ann and Gabriel were already inside. Once inside, Karen shook her head at me.

"You're the only person I know with two lesbian dancing stories."

FORTY-SEVEN

The next day, it rained. It wasn't a polite wishy-washy rain that stops by but doesn't overstay its visit. This was an overbearing, obnoxious Pennsylvania rain. It was an unrelenting, biblical rain that doesn't care whose feelings it hurts and it was all my fault. God was punishing me for my incredible stupidity. I didn't really believe that but I sort of did. Each time I was splashed by cars on my way to work, I thought, "This is what I deserve."

"Holy shit, Stick," Keith said when he saw me, "Did you swim here?"

The week before Keith had begun mocking my skinniness by calling me "The Stick." That's the funny thing about insults. When he'd say things like "When you lift your arms, what radio stations can you pick up?" I got a kick out of it. It meant I'd been accepted. When Drake called me "Scarface", all that meant was that Drake was an asshole.

After everyone arrived, Keith gathered us together.

"We can't cut grass today, we'll have to stay here." While it was true that no one can cut grass during a monsoon, there was nothing preventing us from spending the day painting dorm rooms, except for one thing. Monday was "grass cutting day." The whole idea of painting dorms on a Monday was too absurd to even be considered.

I wished we had. It was more painful doing nothing. We sat around, told a couple of stories, read the paper, a few card games broke out but the day would not end. I could see why prison inmates are punished by having their work privileges taken away. Even

Keith's insults lacked their usual bite. Finally, at 3:30, we were re-leased on our own recognizance.

I got something to eat with the twenty bucks Fitzhugh lent me then went to Jelinak's class. He lectured us about sexual symbolism in dreams. I wasn't in the mood. Any possibility of sex in my future had disintegrated the day before. In the past few months, I had made two attempts at winning women. One relationship ended with me blood-ied and in a dumpster and the other left me humiliated on a suburban street. Just once, couldn't he lecture us on the latency period?

I stopped off at a movie theater on my way home. I was hoping to stave off my loneliness but buying one ticket only reinforced those feelings. It was a Swedish film about how life has no meaning. I couldn't have agreed more. When I came out, the rain had finally moved on. I entered my apartment around ten and nearly tripped over Karen's shoes.

When I saw the shoes, I moved slowly, fearfully towards the living room. I say fearfully because I was afraid that I might be wrong, that maybe the shoes didn't belong to Karen Crespi but there she was. She was sitting next to Fitzhugh on the couch in my living room.

I stood at the living room entrance looking at her. She had a half-smile, her wise ass smile. It was the face she wore when a wise ass comment was about to emerge.

"So, I understand you're quite taken with my aunt Karen." See what I mean?

"That was your aunt?" I asked maintaining a respectful ten-foot distance.

"It just so happens," she explained, "That my Uncle Vince (I call him "Vinny") got remarried about ten years to a fetching widow named 'Karen.'"

"That's a shame," I said, "I thought she and I had the makings of something special."

She let out one of her belly laughs, a big one. God, I love that sound.

I smiled while she laughed. It should have been a romantic moment. It might have been if not for the forty-five year old man in sweatpants sitting next her with a half-eaten piece of key lime pie in front of him reeking of marijuana.

"Your family must think I'm nuts."

"A little bit," she replied.

She laughed again prompting Fitzhugh to giggle ruining the moment.

"My uncle called us yesterday morning and invited us over to see the sign in his front yard. We didn't know what the hell he was talking about but he insisted that we come over. They only live a few blocks away so we piled in the car and drove over."

I cringed and slumped into the chair across from them. I could feel my ears turning red.

"Did everyone have a good laugh at my expense?"

"Not really. No one knew what to make of it. My Dad wanted to know who did it. I told him I had a few suspects."

"Oh, really?"

"Yeah, I narrowed it down to either you or Drake. It's hard to replace a ring speed like mine."

I laughed now. I don't have the infectious laugh that she does. I have the high-pitched nasally laugh of a loner. I'm like the guy in the movie theater who laughs when no one else does.

"I can never meet your family now. I'd be too embarrassed."

She mulled this over. "

They'll get over it, although my uncle is thinking of challenging you to a duel."

Fitzhugh was asleep now. He wasn't snoring per se but he was releasing long, gurgily breaths.

"I brought your stuff," she said, pointing to two bags in the corner. One was my overnight bag and the other a plastic bag filled with a hammer and nails, a roll of white paper and a can of red spray paint.

"Good thing," I said, "I'm going to need that stuff. I spotted an attractive elderly woman on my way home tonight."

She laughed again and Fitzhugh opened and then closed his eyes.

"Maybe we should go in the other room," I suggested.

"Oooh, aren't you smooth with the ladies" she replied leading me to my bedroom.

We sat down on the mattress and didn't say a word for a minute. It occurred to me that she was dressed up. I was used to seeing her in a sweatshirt or a tee-shirt or a cashier's smock. She was wearing what appeared to be a new blouse and a new skirt. It was the first time I'd ever seen her with make-up. She was trying to look pretty and she was succeeding.

The sex was not my best effort. Our separation had made me over-anxious and well, no one wants to hear my excuses. I figured I could make it up to her a few minutes later.

"I have to go," she said.

"Can't you stay the night?"

"No," she said putting her skirt back on, "I'm living at home. My parents have this rule against me spending the night with weirdos who leave signs in old ladies' front yards."

We were both standing now.

"When will I see you again?"

"Tell you what, how 'bout if I leave you my phone number and you call me and we can go out to dinner or the movies, that sort of thing?"

"I don't have a car." "I do."

She was all dressed now. "I love you" I said.

"Well, well, well" she said flashing her best wise ass smile, "I'll bet you say that to all the Karen Crespis."

FORTY-EIGHT

The only thing we kept from my parents' house was the box with my mother's notebooks. Truth be told, we could have used some of the furniture. After all, I'm a teacher living on a teacher's salary. What am I doing turning down free stuff?

Some of the furniture we sold to the people who bought the house, a young couple like us, just starting out. Some stuff we sold at a yard sale. Whatever was left, we just threw out. (My mother's faded red chair was the first thing to go) I just didn't want to hold on to all those bad memories.

The box was different. The box was the key to unlocking my past. It was my Rosetta Stone. I hoped that the box would help me finally understand the woman I'd spent almost my entire life with and yet, whose innermost thoughts remained a mystery to me.

The sheer volume of her writing was overwhelming. It appeared she added an entry each day for twenty five years. She hadn't. This was one of my first discoveries. She didn't write each day, she wrote five days a week. She took weekends off which leads me to believe she didn't write on the days my father was around. He probably never knew that the diaries existed.

Major then Colonel Philbin only kept a journal during the war years. Even during interviews later in life, he spoke almost exclusively about the Civil War and his experiences as a soldier. He didn't discuss moving to the North after the war and how he was able to make a fortune in business creating his own textile fiefdom. He assumed people wouldn't find that part of his life interesting, a rare instance of an egomaniac selling himself short.

Philbin's journals cover a period of not quite four years. Some entries are dozens of pages long giving historians eye witness accounts of the battles of Wilderness and Petersburg. Pages upon pages are filled with vitriolic tirades about Abraham Lincoln and the "abolitionist agitators." Others are sentimental waxings about his men and his home state of North Carolina. There are several gaps of a week or more with no writings including a three and a half month span after he lost his hand at Gettysburg. All told, his work encompassed three full journals.

My mother filled thirty one and a half notebooks. I decided to start at the very beginning and slog my way through, not missing a word. I was as obsessed as she was. At night, when my wife would pop a movie into the VCR, I'd sit at the kitchen table and polish off five or six months of my mother's life. When I should have been grading papers I'd lie in bed with a pillow propped behind my back reading about the winter of '62 or the summer of '74. I'd take a notebook to the park with Gabriel and while he made a friend and ran around, I'd sit on a bench learning about myself at the same age. One Mom asked me what I was reading and I replied, not untruthfully, "A mystery."

My name came up a lot.

"Rory cries a lot and he has a rash. I think his rash is making him cry. I am so tired. I wish he would stop crying. He wakes me up in the middle of the night. I try to ignore him but he won't stop. I wish I never had Rory."

That one kind of jumped out at me. The passages were so repetitious and unvaried there probably isn't another living soul who would find them interesting. Sometimes I would read three or four months of entries before I learned something new. Here was a good one, "Rory's friend Derek came over today. He looks so much like George."

There were other comments along the same lines.

"Derek loves brownies the way George used to."

George is mentioned frequently in every notebook. Here's an example, "Fed some ducks today with Rory. George used to like to feed the ducks. I think that Rory and George would have been friends. I know Rory would have liked George. Everyone liked George."

My wife's theory is that my mother suffered from survivor's guilt. Her little brother George died at twenty-one. She kept living, went to college, married and became a parent. George didn't make it but she did. It just didn't seem fair.

George was not her only obsession. She wrote again and again of how I "hated" her. Here's a snippet from an entry dated "November 18th, 1964 – Rory yelled at me when I gave him a bath. He hates me." November 18th, 1964 was two days before my second birthday. I didn't hate my mother. I hated baths. Here's a good one from when I was 19 months old, "When it started to rain we left the playground and Rory yelled at me."

She often expressed the fear that she wasn't up to the task of being a parent.

"The baby has cried every single day. The doctor is no help."

"The baby just stares at me. What am I doing wrong?"

"I don't know how to act around the baby. I have no idea what I'm doing."

Maybe she wasn't crazy.

She was often unkind to my father, "Walter has another one of those ugly sties in his eye. Why does he get those? The baby cries when Walter sings to him. His singing is so bad the baby cries even harder."

I laughed out loud at this last one annoying my wife who was trying to sleep next to me.

Most of my father related parts were less funny.

"I told Walter we never should have had Rory."

"I hate Walter and I hate Rory."

"I wish I could do it and see Walter's face when I came home."

I have to admit I was a little slow on the uptake. The "it" she spoke of was ridiculously obvious yet my mind chose to block it out as long as it could before I finally had to face facts. The "it" was suicide and I could no longer pretend that it could be something else. For more than twenty years, all my mother thought about was killing herself. When she would sit and stare straight ahead and demand total silence it was this and this alone she was contemplating. Entries that ended with, "I came close today" and "Rory made me so mad today I wanted to do it" became painfully clear what was on her mind.

Yet, it occurred to me that all I had learned was that she "thought" about suicide…a lot. I didn't have proof that she had actually gone through with. It was still possible that my father told me the truth and that my mother had died of heart failure. Plenty of men on death row die before they walk the green mile. I had eight notebooks to go when I made my discovery. I was determined to plow ahead but I wanted to make sure I was right first. Before I did anything else I had to find out for sure if she had really gone through with it.

FORTY-NINE

We'd usually meet at the Colonel. The statue was centrally located so if I was coming from class or from painting a dorm room or from the lower campus maintenance garage it was just easier to meet there. Sometimes, Karen would be waiting for me and sometimes, I'd...well, I guess most of the time she'd be waiting for me now that I think about it.

We'd meet about three or four times a week. On Mondays and Wednesdays, I came directly from Jelinak's class. Karen, like all psych majors at Philbin, was in awe of Jelinak. His mind was obsessed with the human mind. His knowledge and enthusiasm for the id, ego, superego and the conscious and unconscious mind were limitless. To this day when I hear the name Sigmund Freud, I picture Jelinak's face.

After each class, he was always surrounded by a small cadre of suck-ups. If he caught my eye, I would wave and he would nod and return to his flatterers. We were like two colleagues who had a one night stand, realized it was a mistake and avoided each other from that day on.

He obviously felt more comfortable around people who hadn't seen him drunk and crying over a bevy of Asian women. Although I was appreciative for all he had done for me I was just as anxious to shun him. When someone has seen you at your low point even if they help you get through it you end up resenting them. You hate yourself for being so helpless and vulnerable and you hate them for witnessing it. Someone whose life was saved by CPR or the Heimlich will thank their rescuer then hope he dies of a heart attack or by choking on a sandwich.

I never told Karen about the night I spent at Jelinak's. It's funny the things I told her and the things I didn't. She admired him so much it would have been mean to spoil that. It would be like showing a small child Santa's mug shot. She found him brilliant and charismatic and full of passion and so he was but then again so was a white supremacist by the name of Colonel Wesby Philbin. People can be many things at once.

Karen was waitressing now, her supermarket job having recently ended. Sometimes we'd go back to my apartment and Fitzhugh would make us dinner. Sometimes we'd go to a restaurant or a movie before we'd end up back at my place. Once or twice, we barely had sex. What I mean is, sometimes, the sex was our first priority and sometimes it was more of an afterthought.

It was during these times I learned things about her I'd never known. She said her Dad had been "a bit of a drinker", which is, of course, code for "a lot of a drinker." She told me about how when she was twelve years old her father had left her mother for another woman, a much younger woman and how it caused her mother to have what people used to call "a nervous breakdown." I don't know what they call it now. For two and a half months, twelve-year-old Karen Crespi had to assume the mantle of a parent. Karen got up early had breakfast and made lunch for herself and her younger sister and got the two of them off to school. Each night, it was dinner for three and Karen would make something for the three of them. They had either spaghetti or peanut butter and jelly for two and a half months.

This was the story. I had plenty of follow-up questions. Who did your grocery shopping? If it was you, where did you get the money? Did you have to do all the laundry, too? Didn't you need to be driven somewhere from time to time? Didn't your mother have any relative or friend that could help out? I didn't ask any of them. Every family has stories that don't completely hold up under scrutiny.

Anyway, after two and a half months, her father returned. It hadn't worked out with the other woman and it didn't take much apologizing for her mother to take him back. Her younger sister was equally grateful to have her Daddy back. Karen was not so forgiving. For years after, every time he left the house to go to work to run an errand, she had a twinge of fear wondering if he'd be coming back. The more she spoke the more I hated his guts.

It's funny, I always seem to forget that other people have screwed up families, too. Growing up, I'd long for the normalcy of other families not realizing that no such thing exists, that my family doesn't own exclusive rights to mental illness, emotional neglect and dysfunction. If you could peek through the locked doors and the drawn curtains of supposedly happy homes you would find alcoholism and infidelity and domestic violence and a host of other maladies. I guess my point is you shouldn't feel too special just because you come from a fucked-up home.

That's not to say there can't be happy endings. Karen claims her father returned from his sabbatical a changed man. Pre-affair, her parents used to engage in frequent loud, sometimes drunken shouting matches that would reduce her mother to tears. Upon his return, he quit drinking and never again raised his voice to her mother. Fueled by guilt, no doubt, he became a doting, loving husband. In fact, Karen describes her Dad as "funny" and "smart" and "sweet."

I told her all my stuff, too; all the stuff about my parents that I never told anyone. I even told her about Diane and my mother with the blind man's stairs. When Karen's eyes would well up, I'd know that was enough for today and I'd change the subject to something lighter. Small doses were the key to my family lore.

The only topic I'd never bring up was Mary Ann. After all, Karen and Mary Ann had been friends. It was Karen who brought Mary Ann to me. It was Karen who drove me to the hospital when Mary

Ann had her miscarriage. It was Karen who I'd told that I was in love with Mary Ann and was going to win her back even after her family had beaten me up.

It was a difficult subject to avoid. One day at work, as we carried in our paint cans and our brushes and tarp, Keith announced, "This one is going to be a pain in the ass." I should have recognized the room. In fairness to me, with all pictures taken down and all the personal effects removed, every dorm room looks exactly the same.

This one did until we entered the bedroom. The wall had been partially sandpapered but bright yellow wallpaper still shown through. Keith shook his head, "Some crazy chick tried to wallpaper her bedroom."

Fear engulfed me. Was this a trick? Did they know I was the accomplice to this "crazy chick?" Were they trying to gauge my reaction? They didn't appear to be and my fear subsided.

I spent the rest of the afternoon scraping off wallpaper and painting over another of my mistakes. I wanted to tell Karen all about it but I couldn't.

I lied to her a couple of times that summer. She kept inviting me to her parents' house for dinner and each time I made up an excuse of why I couldn't make it. For one thing, the last time I met my girlfriend's parents was last Easter and they ended up reenacting the Passion Play with me playing the part of Jesus. The real reason, of course, was the stupid sign. I thought when I made the "I love you, Karen" sign and hung it in her yard her parents would think it was cute. Then after hanging it in the wrong yard and getting a little distance on the whole debacle I felt ridiculous.

"My birthday is next Tuesday and my parents are taking me to dinner. They want you to come."

"Oh, I have a test the next day in my psych class. Maybe you and I can go to dinner the next night."

She was onto me.

"You're going to have to meet them eventually."

"Oh, no, it's not that, it's just that I have this test."

"Uh-huh."

Her Dad was an old abusive, drunken philanderer and yet, I was too ashamed to meet him.

FIFTY

When I discovered the "it" was suicide I didn't tell my wife. I don't keep a lot from her. Normally, there really isn't anything to be secretive about. It's not like I'm leading a double life. I've never had any affairs or close calls. I'm not interested in anyone else and to my knowledge no one is interested in me.

This was different. She already knew my grandfather committed suicide if I told her I thought my mother did, too, well, it would look like a family tradition. Ernest Hemingway's father and grandfather committed suicide and everybody knows what happened to him. I just didn't want her to think I was next.

Besides, why would I trouble her with something I didn't know for certain to be true? It was just a theory I had that my mother had killed herself. I didn't have any proof. Until I knew for sure there was no need to mention anything to anyone.

I get home early from work most of the time and one day being safely all alone I called the Addison Police Department. I should have planned ahead what I was going to say. The conversation went like this:

"Addison Police Department"

"Um, yes, I was wondering if you could help me?"

"What is your name, sir?"

"Rory Collins"

"What is this concerning, Mr. Collins?"

"Um...a...a possible suicide"

"Are you thinking of committing suicide, Mr. Collins?"

See what I mean? This was exactly what I didn't want. I didn't want people thinking that I was contemplating suicide.

"No, I think she already did."

He got a little panicky when I said that.

"What's your address, Mr. Collins? We'll send a car right over."

"No, no, my mother died seven years ago. I think she killed herself. I just want to know for sure."

He calmed down.

"So you think that your mother killed herself in Addison seven years ago?"

"Yes, sir."

He was quiet for a moment.

"I wasn't on the job then. My sergeant…Sergeant Tobin probably knows all about it. He's in court right now, could I have him call you back?"

"Sure, sure," I gave him the number, "Could he call me back to-morrow around this time?"

Sergeant Tobin called me back an hour and a half later. My wife answered. "Sergeant Tobin from the Addison Police Department," she said handing me the phone. So much for keeping it a secret. It's a good thing I don't have affairs. With my luck, my mistress would call and spill the beans to my wife before I ever got laid.

I took the phone into the bedroom.

"Thank you for calling me back, Sergeant. I was wondering about my mother's death…Helen Collins in March of '82."

"What about it?"

"Was it a suicide?"

"Rory, what do you want to know that for?"

"I just have to know," He sighed, "It's a matter of public record."

Neither of us spoke for a few seconds until he finally gave in, "Yes, the M.E. ruled that it was a suicide."

It hurt me to hear that. He was telling me what I already knew and I wasn't even close with my mother, yet, it stunned and hurt me to hear that. I cleared my throat trying not to convey any emotion. I sat down on the bed.

"Were you at the scene, Sergeant?"

"Yes, Rory," he was very paternal, "We don't get much of that around here. It's a small town. We were all there."

"What happened?"

"Rory, I don't think you need to hear the details."

"Please, Sergeant, it's important." "She…ah…"

Now he cleared his throat, "She killed herself in the bedroom with a shotgun."

"And my father found the body?"

"Yes, he came home several hours later and found the body. He called us."

"How was my father when you got there?"

"Rory," he said not quite yelling at me but scolding me nonetheless, "his wife just killed herself. He was quite upset. We had to have a doctor had to sedate him."

I fought back some tears while he continued, "When people commit suicide it's no one's fault but their own. There is nothing you or anyone else could have done. There is no reason to feel responsible."

I got the feeling this was part of his training. He said a few more things along the same lines but I had stopped listening. I thanked him for his time and hung up.

The image of my father haunts me. He comes home from work to find the love of his life has blown her head off. There must have been blood everywhere. How was he able to regain his equanimity when I saw him two days later?

I was staring at the floor trying to process this new information when my wife came in. "Why is a police sergeant calling you?"

I hesitated.

"Don't tell me you've been knocking off banks again. You know I don't approve."

I didn't laugh. I moved over on the bed so she could sit next to me. Reluctantly, suspiciously, she did so. I told her that in the course of reading my mother's diaries I discovered she had contemplated suicide and I wanted to find out what happened.

"Why didn't you tell me?"

"I am telling you"

"Why didn't you tell me when you found out?"

This was exactly what I was trying to avoid. Why couldn't Sergeant Tobin have called me back the next day like I asked him to? I said specifically, "Please have him call me back tomorrow at this time. Why doesn't anybody fuckin' listen? I looked down at the floor.

"I didn't want you to think that I was thinking about killing myself"

"Are you?"

Why does everyone keep asking me that?

"No, no, of course not"

"You better not."

It took me a while to convince her I would never consider such a thing. She didn't seem entirely convinced.

So now I knew for certain that I was right. My mother had committed suicide. I still had eight notebooks to go through to find out why.

FIFTY-ONE

"How 'bout this Sunday?" Karen asked.

"How 'bout this Sunday?" I replied, having no idea what she was getting at.

"How 'bout this Sunday you come over to my house for dinner and meet my family?"

Now, of course, I didn't want to do that but there is one thing I neglected to mention. She had just gotten naked and I had just gotten naked. She chose that moment on purpose. She had somehow figured out that when we were both naked I tended to be pretty agreeable to whatever she had in mind. This was no exception

"Great," she said, sliding on top of me, "I'll pick you up at one."

In the final days of the Civil War, Philbin's journal entries became irrational. He refused to accept what was becoming increasingly clear to the rest of the Confederate army and the citizens of the states in rebellion, the war was lost. He was like a small child hoping that a dying grandparent will suddenly become all better. Philbin convinces himself that "at any moment" England or France or both will suddenly intercede on the Confederacy's behalf. He even envisions a scenario where Sherman's brutal march prompts a wave of sympathy in the North forcing Lincoln to accept the Southern partition.

I know just how he felt. I was equally desperate to be saved by some kind of Deus Ex Machina. I wished Karen's car would break down, her mother would get the flu or her Dad would get hit by a bus. Okay, the last one was a bit much, but the point is, I really did not want to go.

I was showered and dressed an hour before she arrived. I paced back and forth from the bedroom to the living room to the kitchen. Fitzhugh was trying to watch footage of an anti-police riot in Argentina and he couldn't really enjoy it with me skulking around. Finally, I heard her car pull up.

I don't know if I'd seen Karen nervous before but she was as bad as me. At red lights, she strummed the steering wheel anxiously. She kept biting and unbiting her lower lip.

"My father," she started to say and then stopped.

"What?" "Never mind, you'll see."

What did she mean by that?

"Are they going to bring up the sign?"

"They might."

I let out a groan.

"What did you expect?"

"Nothing," I said, "Just drop me here at the corner."

It's times like these that celibacy looks appealing. Sure, monks have to live in a monastery, sleep on hard beds, eat bad food and spend hours every day in prayer but they never have to meet their girlfriend's parents. A fair exchange.

She drove past the motel I stayed in with my spray can and my roll of paper. I'd already broken my own personal record for cringing and we weren't even at her house yet. She pulled into the driveway of a modest Cape Cod similar to her Aunt Karen's house. We headed through the side door, "Relax," she said, as much to herself as to me.

Her mother greeted us in the kitchen. She was taller than Karen and wider. Her hair was a shade of red not found in nature and she had heavy bags under her eyes. "Is this what Karen is destined to look like someday?" I wondered. Good Lord, I hope not.

While shaking her Mom's hand, her Dad slunk into the room. He was short with thinning black hair and dark glasses and Karen's face. In fairness, I suppose she had his face since he had it first.

"This must be Charlie," he said, "Or is it Sam? Karen has so many boyfriends I can't keep them straight."

"Don't embarrass her, Bill. You'll have to ignore my husband's jokes."

I did my best.

Unlike Mary Ann's father, Karen's Dad wasn't a handsome man but you couldn't help but spot his charm. Like my scar, it was the first thing you noticed about him. He had a big smile that seemed to be just for me. When I spoke his eyes never left mine and he would nod and bite his lip in a manner that seemed to say, "I know just how you feel. Even if no one else does, I do." As we sat at dinner he would tease me from time to time and put his hand on the back of my neck and give it a playful squeeze. I was the son he never had, but I didn't fall for it.

While her mother showed me pictures of Karen as a baby and a toddler and a first communicant, her father told me anecdotes about her as a little girl, stories about kindergarten and the tooth fairy and dropped ice cream cones. They were supposed to be amusing and they probably were but the whole time he spoke I kept picturing him in a motel room with his secretary or whoever it was he ran off with while little Karen Crespi sat looking out the window waiting for him to come home. He couldn't get it through his thick skull that we would never be friends.

Mary Ann's father understood the rules and he didn't. With Mary Ann's Dad the onus was on me to win him over. He was the customer and I had to peddle my wares to him. Karen's Dad had it all wrong. He was trying to sell me on what a great guy he was. He knew he was funny and warm and people instantly liked him and he seemed to grow frustrated when my eyes never smiled back at his.

Karen was just as annoyed as I was. She had tried to be a good sport. She had feigned laughter early in the day but as the afternoon wore on, her patience began to thin. I noticed after each of his jokes or stories she smiled less and less. Towards the end of the meal, she barely spoke and I could see the anger beneath her pleasant façade.

Her father began to sulk or at least pout. He began to suspect I knew the real him and therefore couldn't like him. His jokes took on a less friendly tone. He was like a struggling stand-up comic turning on a tough crowd.

"So Rory, what are your plans after college?"

It was a sneaky way of asking, "What do you want to be when you grow up?"

"I don't know yet."

"Oh," he said, holding back a grin, "I thought you wanted to be a writer. I've read some of your work. It's very concise and to the point."

He had held back with the cracks about the sign until late in the day when the battle hung in the balance.

"Dad," Karen said softly, "You promised you wouldn't."

When it came time for dessert, he made one last attempt at winning me over. He did the old joke of cutting a small piece of cake and then pretending to take the rest, her mother and sister laughed but I didn't. Karen found him even more annoying than I did. I saw the hinges on her jaw tightened.

"It's okay, "I wanted to say, "We're almost done."

After dinner we sat at the table chatting until there was that inevitable lull that signals the end of the evening. "I should get Rory back," Karen said and we all got up from the table. I thanked her mother for a delicious meal and waved good-bye to her little sister. Her father and I shook hands like two political opponents who had earned each other's begrudging respect after a long and nasty campaign.

After Karen and I jumped in the car and closed the doors I breathed a sigh of relief. "That was the worst meal I've ever had," Karen said, backing out of the driveway.

I chuckled. "Well, at least it's over."

As she turned onto the next street she suddenly whirled on me, "What the hell is wrong with you?"

"Wait? You're mad at me?" I asked, feeling sucker-punched.

"Oh, you figured that out, did you?" She said, driving faster than necessary. "How could you do that to my father?"

"I didn't do anything."

"You didn't laugh at any of his jokes."

"How is not laughing at someone's jokes doing something to them?"

"I would never do that to your father."

Neither of us said much the rest of the way. She turned the radio on after the tension became unbearable.

"Do you want to come in?" I asked when she pulled up in front of my apartment.

"I'm kind of tired," she said and she gave me her cheek when I went to kiss her good night.

I knew meeting her parents was a bad idea.

FIFTY-TWO

Just before I left for college, I began having fun with the silent treatment. By this time, my mother had not only completely stopped talking to me she completely ignored me altogether. For instance, if I said, "Pass the salt" she wouldn't pass the salt even though she could have done so without violating the rules of the silent treatment as mandated by the Geneva Convention.

So it was more than just the silent treatment, it was as if I didn't exist. She pretended not to see or hear me and yet at lunch time she'd still make two sandwiches and pour two glasses of milk. It was the most irrational silent treatment in the history of silent treatments.

I began having fun by pretending she was speaking to me. While we sat at the kitchen table at lunch time eating our sandwiches and drinking our milk, I'd turn to my mother and say, "Anything happen in the news today?" Then, I'd wait a few seconds and say, "An earthquake? Where?" Then, I'd pause and say, "Guatemala, really? Did anyone die?" Then I'd wait again and say, "That many? How awful."

Or, after a particularly long silence I would burst out in hearty laughter. "Funny story, Mom" I'd say, shaking my head. "I'll have to remember to tell my grandchildren that one. Of course, I won't tell it as well as you."

It was all very witty and amusing and I entertained the hell out of myself. The day before I left for school I was doing it again when she put her sandwich down. She was sitting to my left and I could see falling from one eye, not the one closest to me but the one farthest away, a single tear. She got up, went to her room and shut the door.

It didn't seem so funny then. I stood outside her room apologizing, "Mom, I'm sorry, I just want you to talk to me."

Nothing.

"Mom, I need to go to college. I just can't stay here. Miss Gillen explained it to you." No response.

"Mom, I can't just stay here forever. I need to go to college so I can get a job."

I even tried opening the door to the room I was never allowed in but it was locked. I started crying, "Mom, I don't want to fight. I don't want to leave this way."

I knew she could hear the tears in my voice but she wouldn't budge. She never did.

That night, my father and I had dinner alone. He brought up a plate filled with food and a knife and a fork. I heard the bedroom door open and close and then he came back down and sat across from me.

"I'm leaving tomorrow and she won't acknowledge me in any way."

"She loves you very much."

That response made no sense, then again, what did in my house?

"How am I going to get to the train in the morning?"

My father didn't drive and my bags were too heavy to lug all the way to the station. "We'll figure something out in the morning."

At breakfast, it was once again just my Dad and me. When I finished my cereal there was still no sign of my mother.

"Should I call a cab, Dad?"

He shook his head.

"That won't be necessary. Your mother is in the car."

I don't know if I'd ever been more surprised by anything in my life. I looked out the kitchen window. There was my mother sitting behind the steering wheel of our car. I hadn't heard the back door or the car door open or close and I was up early. Had she been sitting there all night?

I put the big suitcase in the trunk while my father took the little one. I got in the back seat. "I really appreciate the ride to the train, Mom."

She ignored me the whole way, pretending she wasn't giving me a ride to the train station. When we got there, I took the big suitcase while my Dad carried the little one. The morning was already hot with August reluctant to give way to September. I leaned in to kiss my mother through the car window but she pulled away.

My Dad bought my train ticket.

"Call us if you need anything."

We shook hands. When I got on the train I should have felt a mix of emotions. I should have felt sad about my relationship with my Mom. I should have felt scared about leaving home for the first time. I should have felt reflective about my childhood ending and my adulthood beginning. I didn't feel any of these things. I felt the way Philbin's slaves must have felt when they were freed in 1864. I felt nothing but the pure joy of freedom.

FIFTY-THREE

Karen and I met at the statue the next night and had it out. I was decidedly at a disadvantage since she knew we were going to fight and I didn't. For some reason, I thought it would have all blown over and we would go back to the way things were and just pretend it never happened. That's the way I operate.

She uses a different system. While I spent the day cutting grass and making the coffee run and going to class she was formulating her arguments and planning her rebuttals to mine. Major Philbin and his men once caught a handful of Union soldiers casually filling their canteens by a stream momentarily forgetting they were part of an invading army and wiped them out. One poor Fed was shot through the neck while urinating against a tree. Karen's attack on me was comparable.

She started out with the premise that I didn't really love her because if I did I never would have treated her father with such disrespect. It was absurd. The whole reason I acted the way I did was because I loved her.

"How could I like your Dad after what he did to you and your Mom and your sister?"

"Don't you think I went through that? Do you think it never occurred to me to hate him for that?"

I didn't have a response to this. Hating her father was the proper course of action. It was the only thing that made sense.

She went on and on about how brave her father was to come back and how he knew the contempt he would have to deal with both from his family and the community as a whole but he came back and dealt with it anyway. She said and I quote, "He earned my forgiveness." I wanted to laugh.

Instead, I pretended to let her win. She was so convinced that she was right I didn't have the heart to set her straight. Besides, I could always hate her Dad secretly. So I apologized profusely like I always do and eventually she calmed down and we went back to my place and had sex. Sometimes you have to be the bigger man.

For the next couple of weeks, I noticed there was some lingering uneasiness between us and her father remained as taboo a subject as Mary Ann. It wasn't until my summer classes were ending and I was getting ready to go home that what Karen referred to as her "abandonment issues" kicked in and she started being nice to me again.

I ended the summer with a B+ in my English class and an A in Jelinak's. I'd gotten an A- or two before in my history classes but never a straight up "A." Did Jelinak still feel sorry for me? Was it a bribe to keep quiet about his drunken, crying jag or his personal fetishes? Or is it possible that I actually grasped the basic concepts of Freudian Psychology? Either way, I'll take it.

In honor of my last day, Keith suggested to the football players that maybe one of them could pick up lunch since I'd done it every day prior. None of them wanted to though so I did it again. I didn't mind really.

The football players were all quitting at the end of the week to start their double sessions. I asked them to say hi to Todd for me, the mere mention of his name prompting a mischievous reverence. When I left, Keith pretended to get choked up. I appreciated the sentiment. A sarcastic tribute is better than none at all.

Karen drove me to the train station. Her tears were legitimate. We made out publicly which was not our style, long, wet, salty kisses. It was an even better send-off than Keith's.

I spent the final four weeks of summer home with my Dad. I was shocked to discover how dull things were without my mother. With my mother gone, there was no one to rebel against, there was no silent treatment to laugh at and no insanity to maneuver around. I was like a superhero with no villain. Who would read that comic book?

Sometimes during dinner, my father would reminisce about my mother. I was glad he said her name first otherwise I would have had no idea who it was he was talking about. He would describe "her beauty" and "her grace." Believe it or not, he once actually said he "missed her laugh." I did, too. I missed it completely. It was a reluctant visitor in our humorless home.

One of the things I love about history is its fluidity. The past changes as much as the present. Alexander the Great and Julius Caesar were revered for centuries until Hitler came along and suddenly "conquerors" were viewed in a different light.

Robert E. Lee found slavery to be an odious institution. Yet, he turned down the chance to lead the Union army because he viewed Virginia as home and sought to protect it from attack. He was seen as noble then and noble now.

At the time of his death, Colonel Wesby Philbin was beloved. His men spoke of his "bravery under fire" and his "natural leadership qualities." Turn of the century politicians lauded his "business acumen" and called him "a Captain of Industry." (Are there "corporals of industry"?)

As historians pored over his journals these qualities began to dissipate and eventually disappear altogether. What remained was pro-slavery ramblings and anti-Lincoln vitriol. Upon further review, his genius for business turned out to be nothing more than the exploitation of immigrants and child labor. Fifty years after his death, he was looked on with disdain and eighty years later he's all but forgotten.

I didn't love my mother during her lifetime. It was only after reading her diaries that my feelings changed. As I studied her life like a biographer I was able to understand why she did what she did. I'm not sure I loved my mother while she was alive but I love her now and five years after her death, I discovered for the first time that she loved me.

FIFTY-FOUR

Three and a half weeks into September, the semester was establishing a certain rhythm. On Thursday nights, Todd would head into town, return with a woman with impaired judgment and I'd have to sleep on the couch in the living room. On Friday and Saturday nights, Karen would sleep over in my room or I'd sleep over in hers. The rest of the time was spent going to class, studying or doing normal college stuff.

One Tuesday afternoon, I sat at my desk trying to avoid eye contact with my history paper. I'd gotten a snack, gone to the bathroom, stared into space and twice opened and closed the window. I had just sat back down when I heard a gentle rapping at the door.

It wasn't Karen's knock. Who was this? I opened the door to find Mary Ann. My roommate Chuck (he's new and not important) must have let her in. I almost didn't recognize her. She was wearing the sunglasses she wore when she wanted to hide her wonky eye. She'd put on weight, not in a bad way in a good way. She was too skinny before. Her boobs were bigger and she wasn't as gangly, she was almost voluptuous.

She pushed her sunglasses on top of her head.

"I have to talk to you."

"Come in".

While I shut the door, she sat on the corner of my bed. I sat back down in my chair and faced her.

"I'm pregnant," she said.

She had gotten my attention with this line once before and it worked just as well the second time.

"With your baby," she added after I had failed to respond outwardly.

"I see," I said in almost a whisper.

"You promised me that we'd have a baby together and that we would get married."

This was true. There was no denying it. Just a few months ago, being the father of her baby was all I wanted. After her miscarriage, I promised her I would get her pregnant again. Together we would wash away the pain of the miscarriage with a new baby. I gave her my word.

"Your father," I said carefully, "Your father and your brothers beat me up. They threw me into a dumpster."

I put extra emphasis on the word "dumpster."

"Why did you tell them? Why did you tell them how we met? How could you have been so stupid?"

"I was drunk. They got me drunk."

Neither of us said anything. She looked around the room.

"Your father would never let us get married," I pointed out. She stared straight at me, "Fuck him," she said.

I don't think I'd ever heard her swear before. It sounded funny coming out of her mouth.

"Do you know what he called me when he came home that night? A disgrace. I'm his little girl and he called me a disgrace...on Easter Sunday."

Naturally, there were tears and she made no effort to hold them back.

I got her a glass of water and some tissues.

"It's definitely your baby, you know," she said between sniffles, "You're the only boy I've ever slept with."

She blew her nose and scooped up some tears with a tissue.

In hindsight, I found her choice of language very telling. She called me "a boy." A minute earlier, she'd referred to herself as "a little girl." Her subconscious mind was correct. We were still a boy and a girl, a boy and a girl who were having a baby together. Again.

"I'm practically a stranger in my own house now. My parents have disowned me, practically. They said two words to me all summer."

I could have given her some tips on how to enjoy the silent treatment if she had just asked. She was crying again. I probably shouldn't have gotten her that glass of water. It allowed her tear ducts to reload.

"I'm sorry," I said, sitting on the edge of my desk, "I'm so sorry."

You have to marvel at Mary Ann. Her father and her brothers may punch and kick you, they may pick you up and toss you into a dumpster and leave you there and yet, you'd end up apologizing to her. It's a gift, really, when you think about it.

I cleared my throat and tried to sound as mature as possible.

"Look, I accept full responsibility. I'll do whatever I can to help you support this baby." She looked up with a surprised expression, "You will?"

"Of course."

She stood up.

"Good, good" she said, "glad to hear it."

She wiped away the last of the tears. "I should go. I have a lot of reading to do and I have a French vocab quiz on Friday."

I nodded. Slowly, she leaned in and kissed me. I sort of kissed back, just for a few seconds mind you, for old times' sake, when the door opened and we broke apart.

"Oh, I beg your pardon," Todd said and he reclosed the door.

Both Mary Ann and I were standing now. Her face was red and I'm guessing mine was too.

"I have to go."

She left and I closed the door. I was back sitting at my desk when Todd reentered. I didn't look up. I was pure guilt from head to toe.

He sat down at his desk. I suddenly became quite engrossed in my history paper. I could feel him looking at me. Finally, I looked back, "What?"

"Nothing," he said in full smirk, "Nothing at all."

FIFTY-FIVE

The next day, I was going over my Ancient Civ notes when Todd burst into our room, "Quick, hide!" Hide? What does he mean, "Hide"? He was out of breath, his forehead glistening with sweat.

"Your girlfriends are coming," he was panting hard, "I saw them at the elevator. They'll be here any second."

"You saw them together?"

"Yes, I ran up the stairs."

He bent over at the waist, placing one hand on my desk.

"How do you know they're coming here?"

He glared at me and then breathed in and out again. He spoke through gritted teeth.

"I just know. They're mad and they're coming here. You have to hide."

There was an angry knock at the front door. Todd gave me a look that said, "See." I hid in the closet.

Up until this point, I'd always thought of Todd as just my roommate even though we had chosen to room together year after year. However, any guy, especially one as sedentary as Todd, who runs up five flights of stairs to warn you that your two girlfriends are coming to get you, well, that's a real friend.

Evan, my other roommate (he's also new and not important) opened the door. There was some low murmuring coming from the next room but I couldn't hear what they were saying. I was, after all, crouching in a closet, my head buffeted by a dozen shirts.

"They're coming," Todd whispered excitedly.

I bit down on my lower lip.

After a few moments, I heard Mary Ann and Karen enter my bedroom. "Hey, what's up?" asked Todd nonchalantly, sitting at his desk.

"Where is he?" Karen asked.

"Who?"

This may not have been the best response.

"Rory," Mary Ann said, "Where is he?"

"He's not here."

"Where is he?"

"I don't know."

"I think you're full of shit," Karen said.

"I do too," said Mary Ann.

As you can imagine my heart was racing. I was in a closet just a few feet away. I could hear every word. My back wanted me to stand up straight. My legs needed a good shake. I closed my eyes and tried not to breathe.

"Why are you sweating?" Mary Ann asked.

"It's hot in here," Todd said, "Aren't you hot?"

"No." "Are you hot?" Mary Ann asked Karen.

They seemed to be quite chummy.

"No."

No one said anything for several seconds, then Todd broke the silence, "Look, he's not here."

Nothing.

"He isn't. You can look around if you want to but he's not here."

"All right," said Karen, "I think we will."

A second later, she opened the closet door. Karen's not too tall so with me hunched over we were eye to eye. There were coat hangers and shirts around my head. I was standing on some sweaters.

"Get out of there," she said.

I was never so embarrassed in all my life and anyone who knows anything about my life knows that's saying a lot. I stepped out of the closet. I arched my back and shook out my legs.

Mary Ann looked over at Todd, "I thought you said he wasn't here?" "

I had no idea he was in there" Todd said.

She turned to me. "What is wrong with you?"

A fair question. "I...I...I just needed some time to think."

"Well, too bad" she said.

"Sit down," Karen chimed in, "We want some answers."

How can an Arab sheik stand having two wives? Every time they have a fight, he gets ganged up on.

I sat down on the bed avoiding eye contact with both of them.

"Look, um..." I started to say, "Wait a second," Mary Ann interrupted, "I think he should leave."

She pointed a finger at Todd sitting quietly in the corner.

"Please can I stay? I won't say a word." Desperate for an ally, I immediately took his side.

"It is his room," I pointed out, "We can't kick him out of his own room." "

Yes, we can," Karen snapped, "Get the fuck out of here."

Under protest, Todd left slowly hoping they would change their minds. Karen shut the door behind him.

The two of them stood while I sat.

"I want to know what's going on," Mary Ann demanded.

"What do you mean?" I asked.

Karen stepped in, "You can't have both of us."

"That's right," Mary Ann said.

Maybe the two of them should be a couple. They seemed to see eye to eye on everything. "You have to choose right now," Karen said.

Personally, I hate confrontations.

I took a moment to carefully craft my response, "I am very fond of both of you."

"Don't give us that," Karen said.

I took a breath and glanced at each of them. They both looked at me with such intensity. I stared at the floor.

"I'm pregnant," Mary Ann reminded me, "With your child."

She made a compelling case. "I'm your girlfriend," Karen pointed out, "Remember, you told me you loved me."

This was also persuasive. Not since Lincoln and Douglas had America seen such skilled debaters.

"Any guy would be lucky to have either one of you," I said.

That really got them mad. Karen threw up her hands in disgust. Mary Ann looked like she wanted to punch me. She wouldn't have been the first in her family to do so.

"All right, all right" I said carefully, "I'll tell you what I'm looking for."

No one moved. "I'm looking for a woman who loves me." "I love you," Mary Ann said right away.

"We both love you," Karen said.

"All right," I said, still not looking up at either one of them, "I want the one who loves me the most."

They both mulled this over.

"Which one is that?" Karen asked.

"Yeah" said Mary Ann.

"I'm not sure," I shrugged.

Karen swore and Mary Ann stomped her foot. It was hard to believe either one of these women loved me, never mind both of them.

"Rory," Mary Ann mumbled, "C'mon."

I put up my hands to placate them.

"I have an idea."

"What, you want us to arm wrestle?" Karen said bitterly.

"No, I'll tell you what. I'll choose whichever one of you can tell me when my birthday is."

There was a brief silence.

"What?" Mary Ann said in disgust.

"That's stupid," Karen agreed.

"No, it isn't," I said, defending myself for the first time.

"I know your birthday is January 13th", I said to Mary Ann, "And I know yours is July 8th", I said to Karen, "because you're important to me. If I was important to you, you'd know when mine is too."

There was a tense moment when they both realized I was serious and these were my terms. I turned to Mary Ann.

"I don't know," she snapped.

I looked at Karen. "November 12th", she said with the hint of a smile. ("Close enough," I decided)

"You got it," I said aloud.

The magnitude of what had just transpired dawned on Mary Ann. She opened her mouth for a second and then scrunched up her face.

"You can't be serious?" "Sorry, but my birthday is November 12th", I lied and shrugged.

"I'm carrying your baby," she yelled, tears falling fast, "Who cares when your stupid birthday is?"

"That was the arrangement. A deal's a deal."

"Yeah," said Karen, "I won."

Mary Ann, turned towards the door with her shoulders convulsing. As she reached the door she looked back, her face, deep red with rage, she growled, "I'm glad my brothers beat you up."

FIFTY-SIX

I got a call from Mary Ann about a week before our baby was born. She had learned some new statistics. Baby boys without fathers were 17% more likely to have gender identification issues. Children in one parent homes were more susceptible to drug and alcohol addiction later in life. That sort of thing. She decided she wanted me to be part of our baby's life and I wanted that as much as she did. I'd show my Dad a thing or two about being a father.

I talked one of my professors into letting me take my last final exam early due to the birth of my child. It was an awkward conversation. I then hopped a train to Ohio and with the help of some of Karen's waitressing money I stayed in a cheap motel. Mary Ann called me a few hours after Gabriel was born. It was a name she picked out and I kind of liked it. Her parents were in the delivery room for the birth but now that they had gone home for the night it was safe for me to stop by and meet my son. I returned to the same hospital where the year before I had entered with a broken nose, cracked ribs and a swollen face. I have fonder memories of this time around.

Guys always talk about the moment they hold their newborn baby and how happy they felt and how magical it is. I felt all that stuff but only later on the train ride home. When I first held that tiny little baby that I had helped create and who I was responsible for from now on, I felt complete and utter terror. I know this sounds dumb but when she put him in my arms my first thought was, 'I've got to do better in school."

Mary Ann took a semester off then returned to Philbin the following September. She explained to me that children of college graduates are 32% more likely to attend college themselves. Her parents set her up with an apartment off campus and a nanny, a middle-aged Albanian lady, to take care of the baby while she was in school and I got to see Gabriel all the time.

Karen and I married four years later. We decided to wait until she finished grad school. She's a psychologist now and she's had a lot to say about select passages from my mother's diaries.

It was a small wedding. Gabriel, in his little suit, was the ring bearer. After walking down the aisle, he greeted me with "I love you, Dad" thus breaking family tradition by not waiting 'til his father was in a coma.

Karen's father gave her away and she practically had to carry him firefighter-style down the aisle. He was a blubbering, quivering mess. However, when it came time for his toast at the reception, he was his old self, "I'm in retail I never give anything away."

Even I laughed at this something Karen took note of.

Fitzhugh came. He was now a chef at a small restaurant in Millwood. He seemed almost happy and only slightly stoned. Jelinak was there, as Karen's guest not mine. He brought a Filipino woman. They seemed serious. Karen's sister was the maid of honor. Three of her bridesmaids went to Philbin with us, two of whom, Karen once brought to my dorm room during her "pimp" phase.

Todd was my best man. Karen thought I was kidding when I told her.

"Seriously, who's it going to be?"

"Todd." "Do you really want him giving the wedding toast?"

I hadn't thought about that and I braced myself when the time came. Karen squeezed my hand, her nails digging into my palm, petrified at what Todd might say in front of her mother, father, grandmother, the other Karen Crespi, her uncle Vince, her sister and various other family and friends.

"Cheers," Todd said, extending his glass and then sitting back down to stunned silence. "That was some tribute" Karen told him later, "You must have practiced all day in front of a mirror."

Karen was still peeved about the bachelor party, another event I'd forgotten about when I appointed Todd best man. Karen and I were home two nights before the wedding when Todd appeared at my door. It was the second time in my life he'd come to abduct me. The first time was with Jelinak, this time, sitting in the front seat of his car was a beautiful black stripper.

"Who's that?" Karen demanded.

"Oh…you mean Tiffany?"

Todd replied as though she had slipped his mind. As if he had hired a stripper, picked her up, drove her to my house and then forgot she was there.

"She's just a friend."

It took me several minutes to convince Karen there was nothing to worry about. Todd then drove us (sans Karen) to a hotel room where a handful of my friends had gathered. Tiffany had remembered her boom box but forgotten her tapes so she had to perform with just the radio on. We clapped and hooted to be polite, trying not to laugh when a commercial came on in the middle of her routine. Afterwards, she offered to perform privately some random acts of kindness. Todd took her up on it. It was Thursday night after all. I declined, having enough casual sexual encounters for one lifetime.

Mary Ann stopped by the reception to pick up Gabriel and wish us well. Thanks to him, she's in my life forever. We live not far away and I see her every Wednesday and every other weekend when I pick him up. She got married recently to a friendly oaf named Roger. The four of us had dinner once. (It was surprisingly pleasant and kind of fun and we never did it again.)

These days, for the most part, I actually enjoy my life. That's the beauty of having a shitty childhood you don't long for an idyllic past.

It fills me with if not joy at least relief to be living in a world free stony silence and paralyzing tension.

I chose the right wife. We go on hikes, we watch our shows and we read many of the same books. Karen loves Gabriel almost as much as I do. The three of us celebrate my birthday every year on November 12th. (I've never corrected her) After we put some money away, we hope to have one or two more just like him.

I've even starting working on a biography of Colonel Wesby Philbin in my spare time. (It's been 40 years since the last good one) Mostly, I spend my days teaching my classes, grading my papers and making my peace with my mother.

FIFTY-SEVEN

When I finally got to the last three notebooks I couldn't stop reading. It was no longer a few minutes here and there. I was like a law student cramming for the bar exam. Until I finished everything else in my life would just have to wait.

I read before school, in the teacher's lounge during school, after school, on the toilet (sorry!) and up until bedtime. I stopped assigning homework because I didn't want to take time away from the diaries to correct it. Karen let me have one full weekend to wrap it up.

Three of the notebooks were almost exclusively about me and cover my high school years and my first year of college including passages like this one: "

Rory didn't eat all his lunch today. We had ham sandwiches left over from the ham we had for dinner on Sunday. We had ham sandwiches and peas and he didn't eat a single one of his peas and he used to love peas. When he was little, peas were his favorite vegetable. It used to be that he didn't like ham. Now he likes ham and hates peas."

I realize how uninteresting these passages are. They aren't even interesting to me and I'm Rory.

During the Diane incident and the subsequent trial, right around the time my dreams changed and become dark and chilling, there is a shift in the tone of her diaries. She no longer rambles on blithely. Suddenly, each entry is no more than a sentence or two. The daily minutia and the major events of my life are described in the same terse manner and given the exact same weight. Each entry is like a telegram conveying a simple message in as few words as possible.

Each one would seem utterly meaningless if you didn't know the events to which they were attached.

"I protected Rory today."

Those four words are from the day she got up in the middle of the night to drive across town to vandalize a teenage girl's home. Here's one from the trial, "I don't know what he sees in that skinny girl." She wasn't so skinny, lady, until you publicly ostracized her for no reason and destroyed her youth. It was at this time that I hated my mother and as it turns out, she hated me back. She stops saying my name and writes entries like this:

"He's too stupid to appreciate what I've done for him."

"I will never speak to him again."

"I despise him."

The notebooks reveal a person completely incapable of remorse. There is no reflection, no expression of regret for mistakes made and never the slightest consideration of the other person's point of view. Karen tells me all of this is consistent with a narcissistic borderline personality.

My father is not mentioned in the final notebook. She writes a lot about her brother George and a lot about me. She talks more and more about "doing it." The suicide talk ramps up from once a week or so, to three or four times a week to eventually, every day. Here's one from November 20th, 1980, "He's eighteen today. I can do it now."

Here's the one from the day I left for college, "I should have done it in front of him. That would wipe the smirk off his face."

It was just as I suspected. It was all my fault. I wept without restraint.

With less than three weeks to go in my mother's life, I stopped reading. I put the last notebook back in the box and shoved it under my bed. I couldn't continue reading now that I knew that not only had my mother murdered herself but that I was an accomplice, a co-conspirator. All I could think about was that if I had just called my mother on her birthday maybe she would have realized that I didn't hate her and maybe she'd still be alive. But I didn't call. I was too busy having sex with a series of unattractive women. I wanted to give myself the silent treatment. I was the worst guy I knew.

At Gettysburg, Philbin lost more than his hand. He lost his dream of being a hero to the victorious Southern army and perhaps, even one day, the President of the Confederacy. It took him four and a half months of agonizing depression before he could re-summon his ardor and return to the battlefield. It took me much longer. For five and half years, I let those last few pages go unread while I slept uneasily just a couple of feet about them.

Twice, we moved and the box moved with us. From time to time Karen nudged me towards it but, I always resisted. Finally, one wintry day with the house to myself, I mustered up the courage to read about the last three weeks of my mother's life. I expected to find a woman on the brink of despair. Instead, the tone of those passages range from matter-of-fact to downright pleasant. She begins reminiscing about George.

"George would start to laugh even before I tickled him."

"George used to yell, 'bread and butter' at bees to scare them away."

She also began to reminisce about me. She begins using my name once more and speaks of me with unmistakable fondness.

"Rory would make me push him for hours on the swing."

"Rory's hair used to get so light in the summer time."

She seemed to remember an idyllic past in both George's and my childhood that I don't think ever existed but for which she longed for just the same.

I braced myself as her birthday approached but all she wrote was "it's my birthday today." She didn't mention me or the fact that I didn't call. Her birthday seemed to be a minor event. Her main focus was the day just three days after her birthday. Here's what she wrote, "George's anniversary is in two days. I'm going to do it then."

"George's anniversary is tomorrow. I'll be with him."

She had decided to kill herself on the same day that her brother had killed himself which was of course the same day their father had killed himself. Her birthday seemed to have nothing to do with it. Something that Karen frequently reminds me.

The last entry is the most illuminating of all.

"I'm going to do it today. I would have twenty years ago if it weren't for Rory."

My mother hated her life. She didn't love her husband. She had no friends. She missed her brother and never got over his death. She felt tremendous guilt that she was still alive and he wasn't. She viewed suicide as a way of reuniting with him. For twenty years she longed to do it. She thought about it obsessively every day. Yet, every day, for twenty years she fought the urge because of me.

Now that I was grown up and out of the house, she could finally do it. She could finally go and be with her brother who she loved so much. She didn't kill herself because of me. It was because of me that she postponed killing herself for twenty years. When she finally did do it, she didn't do it in front of me the way her father had. She waited until I was far away and wouldn't be the one to find the body. Now, if that's not love, then I don't know what love is.